Caught
in the
Mix

Caught in the Mix

Candice Dow

KENSINGTON PUBLISHING CORP.
http://www.kensingtonbooks.com

DAFINA BOOKS are published by

Kensington Publishing Corp.
850 Third Avenue
New York, NY 10022

All Kensington titles, imprints and distributed lines are available at special quantity discounts for bulk purchases for sales promotion, premiums, fund-raising, educational or institutional use.

Special book excerpts or customized printings can also be created to fit specific needs. For details, write or phone the office of the Kensington Special Sales Manager: Kensington Publishing Corp., 850 Third Avenue, New York, NY 10022. Attn. Special Sales Department. Phone: 1-800-221-2647.

Dafina and the Dafina logo Reg. U.S. Pat. & TM Off.

ISBN 0-7582-1053-1

First Kensington Trade Paperback Printing: June 2005
10 9 8 7 6 5 4 3 2 1

Printed in the United States of America

Acknowledgments

Above all, I would like to thank GOD for giving me this gift and planting the desire in my heart to make it known. You have truly shown me favor.

To my parents: Mommy, you have been the best mother a girl could ask for. Thanks for never judging me, always believing in me, and always listening to me. You are the best and words could never express how much I love and admire you. Daddy, thank you for always being there, loving and supporting me through all my transitions. At times, you were the only one who understood. Thank you for believing in me and inspiring me to follow my dreams.

To my sister, Lisa. From as far back as I remember, you have always been the rock for me to lean on. I owe so much of who I am today to your strict guidance. You are truly the wind beneath my wings. I hope I will always make you proud. Thank you for your unconditional love. Also, for giving me the best nieces in the world, Morgan and Maccy. Although you girls try to drive me crazy, you are my inspiration. Everything I do is for you. To my nieces: Ashley, Tatijana, Carlisia, Akerah, Nia, and Asia. I love you all so much. To my own auntie, Odie, you have always been my biggest fan. You have served so many roles in my life and never have you complained. I love you and I am so happy that you belong to me.

To my brothers, Omar and Antwan, I love y'all. My little sister, Crystal, you are such a little lady. Your wisdom never ceases to amaze me. Angie, thanks for always letting me know how special it is to be a Dow. Much love. Dee-Jay, thank you for loving me and adopting me as your mother.

My cousin, Tara, you are such a positive person and I love you for that. I cannot tell you how often your words of encouragement keep me going. You always see the brighter side. That is such a rare quality. Never, ever lose sight of that. The world would be a better place if more people were like you. Chip, I love you, cousin. To my very first partner in crime, Kisha, I love you and thanks for all the memories.

Anika, claiming someone as a best friend was something I never subscribed to, until God gave me you. Girl, I love you. Who would ever think the world was big enough to hold the both of us? I truly appreciate your sense of humor and zest for life. Thanks for being my "hype girl" and I will always, always be yours. Ride or die for life!

Sham, my soror and friend. You are such a good person. Our morning talks mean the world to me. No matter how far fetched I am, you always find purpose in my words. Wherever I am, I know that I can always depend on you. Your friendship is so invaluable. Thank you.

And to all my line sisters and the sorors of Alpha Kappa Alpha Sorority, Inc. I love you. Thanks for teaching me the true meaning of sisterhood and the rewards of perseverance. I definitely needed it!

To my girls in the *Sex and the City* crew: Tanika, Kendra C., Kendra M., Tasman, and Ona. And my other good girlfriends: Angelique, Martha, and Robyn. Thanks for all the years of girl talk and validating that women do get along! Tia, I am so happy you gave me a deadline on this project. That was exactly what I needed. Thank you so, so much. Toya, you believed in me when this was a mere fantasy. I promised every week to get focused and you never got tired of hearing it, even when I had yet to write a sentence. When I was FINALLY done, you were there to read and edit every word. That meant so much to me. Nicole, thanks for willingly offering your editing touches, as well. I sincerely appreciate you. You really did a great job, and I love you both.

To my good work friends, all of whom, have endured my endless conversations while supposedly working. Tiffany Amos, Latosha Singleton, Angelina Seldon (thanks for the title), Melissa Johnson, Jennifer Graves, Lori Cady, Dionne Whitaker-Moore, Mariama Black, Kim Mason, Marcellus Major, Dob Ward, Rob Gaither, Vernell Savage, Vernessa Alexander. And to any of my coworkers that I failed to list, if you have been a victim of my drama, thanks for your listening ear.

To my agent and friend, Audra Barrett. What a perfect match! I am so blessed to have you on my side. You are the best!

Thanks to everyone at Kensington who made this dream a reality. Especially my editor, Karen Thomas, and her assistant, Nicole Bruce.

To all the members of the Love Crowd Christian Light Church, thank you all for your love, support, and prayers.

And to anyone that I may have forgotten, I love you and thanks for touching my life.

THE PRESENT

PROLOGUE

I sat on the hotel bed and looked into the Victorian-styled mirror. The ten pounds that had recently evaporated from my body reflected as a skeletal figure. What used to be referred to as luscious lemons lay limp and lifeless in my push-up bra. The wide elastic band on my white pantyhose pressed into my belly, exposing the protruding bones that hid beneath my skin. I blew air into my jaws, stuck my breast out, trying to create the illusion of a fuller me.

I combed my hair down; then I pinned it up, desperately attempting to expose my golden highlights. After I applied my makeup, I paced around the hotel room, from the bathroom to the window, rubbing my sweaty palms. Finally, I sat on my hands, trying to soak up the anxiety flowing from them. I rehearsed what I'd written over and over in my head. "Devin, I have loved you my entire adult life."

My mind would then freeze. What was I supposed to say next? My dress lay on the adjacent bed, waiting to be draped upon my body. My eyes watered as I visualized the episode about to begin. I dried my tears with the tips of my fingers. Without further delay, I grabbed my dress and began to step into it. My body trembled like an alcoholic in need of a shot. Wisdom began invading my thoughts, telling me to stay in my room and forget about the whole thing.

With my equilibrium disrupted, I dropped the dress and lay back on the bed. I looked at the alarm clock. Five-fifty. Ten minutes until the verdict. With each flickering nerve in my body, I rummaged up the strength to slide into my dress. I took one final glance in the full-length mirror on the bathroom door.

With enough confidence to feed a fish, I opened the door. I slammed it. I began pacing around the room again, pounding my fist, praying aloud. Three minutes before the procession and still, I contemplated. Afraid to move. Afraid to stay.

I rushed to the door and down the hall. With each step, I found the courage to continue. Baby steps converted into brave strides. Reluctance disguised as determination.

To avoid being seen by the incoming guests, I slipped into the stairwell. My three-inch heals clicked loudly as I galloped down four flights. When I reached the ballroom floor, my heart thumped anxiously. I stood there. Anticipation boiled inside of me in the form of indigestion. I climbed onto my tiptoes and peeped through the tiny windowpane. The bridesmaids, dressed in beautiful cranberry velvet gowns, hustled past. I quickly ducked.

I prayed desperately that my insanity was in vain. I hoped he would be the one to call it off.

Then, as if summoned, I heard his voice approaching. I began to nibble on my lips. I walked in five-step circles and mumbled, "Oh, my God. He's really here. Oh, my God."

He and his best man stopped directly in front of the door which I stood behind. Oblivious to my surveillance, they continued to talk.

Jason, his best man, kidded, "Yo, I 'on believe you crazy enough to go through with this."

Devin smiled. "Man, I'ain afraid of commitment. You know that."

"You right. You been on lockdown forever."

Devin laughed. "Ain't nothin' wrong with that. When you find something good, you hold on to it."

Jason seemed to meditate on Devin's philosophic words. "True. True."

Then another groomsman walked up. "You ready, dawg?"

"Man, as ready as I'm 'gon be."

Expressions of gratitude lurked in his eyes. There was confidence in his words, joy surrounding his presence. Doubt began plaguing me. My eyes shifted from mouth to mouth. Hoping. Praying. Maybe just maybe someone would give me one reason to run back to my room.

His parents walked up, and his mom kissed his cheek. Thin red lips printed meticulously on his flawless caramel skin. She held his face between her slim, pale hands. Pride written vividly on her leathery face, she simply shook her head at her baby boy. He blinked rapidly, attempting to restrain the emotions, the unspoken words. His father shook his hand and patted him on the back.

Trapped in a virtual insane asylum, my hands pressed flat against the door. Inwardly, I screamed loudly, but no one heard my cry. I banged frantically, but no one acknowledged the commotion. How could I stop it? How could I lose the only man I've ever loved?

He and Jason stood in silence for a moment. Jason asked, "Do you ever . . . ?"

Devin's eyes stretched, as if he awaited the question. He anxiously asked, "Do I ever, what?"

Jason waved his hand. "Never mind, man. It's your wedding day."

Devin paused for a moment and said, "You think I'm making a mistake. Don't you?"

The expression on Jason's face obviously confirmed Devin's question. Then the minister called for them. Jason shook Devin's hand. "Man, I wish you the best. It's too late to question it now. It's that time."

They embraced. Jason walked rapidly in front of him. Devin took two slow, concentrated steps. With the future of our relationship lying solely in my hands, I yanked the door open and loudly whispered, "Devin . . . Devin."

I

CLARK

When I met Devin, I knew he was the man for me. It was the first day back from summer break. My friends and I were sitting on the yard drinking and talking trash. After three years at Hampton University, we were all exhausted. Tired of one-night stands. Tired of lies. Tired for the sake of being tired. We were ready for relationships.

I added my drama into the discussion: "I'm sick of wasting my time. Maybe I'll meet my husband at work. 'Cause nothing's down here! I have a *Don't Go There* list. If you need a copy, let me know. I'm giving them away, so you don't have to waste your time. I even have the reasons beside the names. Too rough. Too big. Too small. Too quick. Let me save you the trouble!"

My friends laughed as I ranted about the infamous list. A few girls sitting nearby scooted closer. One of the intruders chimed in, "I'll give you five dollars for that list!"

Her cohorts nodded. With an attentive audience at hand, I continued, "Either it's Hampton, or it's me. It has to get better."

Another intruder asked, "Isn't your name Clark?"

Had she heard something negative about me? Immediately prepared to defend myself, I planned to say, "And what about Clark?"

Instead, I took the subtle approach. "Yeah."

She smiled. "I think I know someone you can't totally rule out yet."

I looked at Ms. Matchmaker and shook my head. Disappointed. Disgusted. Disgruntled. "Girl, trust me, I'm not even wasting my time anymore."

Despite my lack of interest, she described him. ". . . He's a sophomore . . ."

Everything prior to that statement I ignored. "Do you know I'm a graduating senior?"

"Yeah . . . and?"

"And . . . I'm not baby-sitting."

"Girl, Devin is all that and a bag of chips." She slapped one of her girls a high five.

"I don't care if he is the entire damn chip factory. I never baby-sat before, and I don't plan on starting any new habits. Okay?"

With my hand in the halt position, I motioned for her to stop joking and move on. She frowned and smacked her orange-painted lips. She shook her head, which was being smothered by bundles of silky fake hair. Anyone associated with this girl was not someone I was interested in meeting.

She quickly walked away, leaving her friends sitting with us. Surprisingly, my shady friends never attempted to drift away from the tacky girls. Oh, yeah, it was probably me who welcomed the intrusive creatures. I shut my big mouth, and we all sat silently. Thinking. Drinking. Wondering. Is there really no such thing as the one?

The back-to-school block party boomed around us. The Greek Organizations stepped and chanted. People laughed, chatted, embraced, and we just looked pitiful. Nothing. No hope. Words too sad to say, we drank more E&J straight, chasing it with a splash of Coke. Single. Drunk. Mary J. Blige's song, "Real Love," pumped from car speakers. Everyone was searching for the same thing.

Ms. Matchmaker trudged toward me, holding hands with the sexiest man I'd seen in all my life. I sat up from my slouching position to admire the fine specimen. Tall, thick, caramel. Short black wavy hair evenly covered his head. Please hand me a drink of water. My body burned all over.

I looked at her girls, baffled. "Is that her man?"

"Naw, that's the guy she was trying to tell you about."

I felt naked. Just as I attempted to hang my head, to repent for my reluctance to meet him, they were directly in front of me. I stood to welcome the introduction.

"Clark, this is my friend, Devin."

Devin extended his muscular arm, tilted his perfectly oval head, and slumped down. I raised my chin. With a voice as clear as the summer sky, he said, "Nice to finally meet you, Clark. I've been trying to get your attention for a long time."

His demeanor was humbling. I continued grasping his hand. "Nice to meet you, too. Can't say I've been trying to get your attention, but you definitely have mine."

As I spoke, I looked him up and down like a hungry bear, conveying with every active body part that I was open as wide as an erupting volcano and willing to hear anything he had to say. Apparently noticing my interest, he smiled. His teeth were aligned like soldiers in the army. As I admired his anatomy, our eyes connected. He stared through me like the lenses of an X-ray camera. I felt paralyzed, heart still, awaiting his diagnosis to determine my destiny. He squinted and gently tugged his bottom lip with his top teeth.

Ms. Matchmaker winked at me and raised her thumb. I responded with a sincere expression of appreciation and approval. She nodded a little, hinting to her friends to give us some privacy. My friends were literally stretched out on the grass. Too much E&J.

"I've never seen you around. Where you been hiding?"

"Well, I only see you in passing. When I'm coming on the yard, you're usually going off."

"So, if that's the case, how did you know you wanted to meet me?"

"April 'ninety-four." He shrugged his broad shoulders and smiled like a little boy who got caught looking under his classmate's dress.

I was voted among the top twelve most attractive girls at the university the previous school year. We all got a month in the school's swimsuit calendar.

I teased, "So, you're just interested in my body. Huh?"

"Naw, I also noticed you're smart, too. You have like a three point eight GPA, right?"

As if I wasn't impressed, "Yeah . . . uh-huh."

"Seriously, I'm turned on by a smart woman. Not to mention, a beautiful sista."

An appreciative grin broke through my pursed lips. "Uh-huh."

"Look, Clark, I'm straight up. Plus, word around campus is you're a no-nonsense kind of girl. You have to come correct or don't come at all. Right?"

I laughed hysterically. "Who told you that?"

"Guys talk. And I'll leave it at that."

I left that one alone. Innocent until proven guilty.

"So, you staying out here much longer?"

I turned to look at my friends, lying out on the grass like homeless alcoholics. "I'm outta here soon as these drunks wake up."

He laughed, apparently enjoying my candid sense of humor. "We should go somewhere and talk."

Talking was the last thing I wanted to do with this man. If we went to my place, the appetite we'd developed for each other would undoubtedly demand to be fed. "Let's go to the lobby of your dorm."

"Why do you think I stay in the dorms?"

I rolled my neck. "'Cause most underclassmen stay in the dorms."

"I'm not your average underclassman."

That comment expanded my curiosity. "So, what are you like?"

With a sneaky chuckle, he said, "Let's go back to my apartment and you'll see."

Offended by his inaccurate assumption, I frowned. He obviously presumed or heard that I was easy.

I said, "What makes you think I want to find out what you're like on the first night?"

I put my hand on my little hip. "I don't kick it like that. And if you think you're gonna get some, you better think again."

He looked down at me, standing an entire foot below, like a principal feeling sympathy for the school bully, obviously recognizing the pain that lived beneath the surface. He lifted my chin with his slightly curved hand.

Innocently he began, "Clark, I don't want to take advantage of you. That's not even my style. I just want to get to know you. I just want you to come over so we can talk. I promise I won't try anything, not even a kiss." He reached out his hand to shake mine. "Deal?"

Not even a kiss? What's wrong with me? Attempting not to reveal my indecisiveness, I smiled and nodded.

His reaction to my temper tantrum was staggering. *Gentle.* I needed that, a man who knows how to love his woman and control the uninvited little girl who lurks inside. He possessed a serious, mature, no-playing-allowed demeanor.

"Clark! Clark!"

As I daydreamed that he might actually be the one to save me, I totally ignored him.

"Yeah, I'm just a little tipsy. What were you saying?"

"I asked you if you were ready to go somewhere where we can talk. It doesn't have to be my place."

I agreed to go to his apartment. He grabbed my hand and guided me toward the parking lot. Holding hands was a bold statement, definitely not a move that the average man at Hampton would initiate. One of them would have suggested that we meet in a particular spot away from the crowd like private detectives, attempting to conceal our intent. Without hesitation, I proudly pushed through the crowd with his fingers intertwined in mine, advertising my new-found treasure.

As he spoke, I noticed an unfamiliar accent. "So, Devin, where are you from?"

"Phoenix."

"Phoenix, Arizona!"

"Yeah. Why do you sound surprised?"

"Because you are the only person I know from Phoenix." I kidded, "I didn't think black people lived there."

He smirked. "Is that right?"

"No, I'm just joking. So, what brings you all the way to Hampton U?"

"You."

Just flatter me. I giggled. "Sure."

"No, honestly. I grew up in a predominately white neighbor-hood, and I wanted to go to college where I could be around my people."

"I can respect that."

He smiled. "I'm glad."

We walked up on a 1993 black BMW 525i. Devin pressed the alarm. I hesitated. Where did he get this nice luxury ride? Trying not to appear too inquisitive, I asked, "Why do you have this mid-night black tint. Are you hiding from someone?" I kidded, "This is why I've never seen you. You've been hiding."

He laughed. "Yeah, it's useless here, but at home I wouldn't survive without tint."

Not survive? I blurted out, "Why?"

"Man, it can get up to 120 degrees in Phoenix."

"Oh, yeah, that's true."

Hopefully that's the only reason for the tint, because in my neighborhood, a BMW with tint spells trouble. I said a quick prayer for safety. He walked to the passenger side and opened my door. Within seconds, he scurried around to the driver's side and jumped in. He looked into my eyes as he put the key into the ig-nition. To alleviate the intensity of the moment, I said, "Play a song for me."

"Just a minute." He fumbled with the widget. "This song is def-initely for you."

Jodeci's "Can I Talk to You" began playing. Blushing shyly, I meditated on the lyrics. Appropriate. Before the song went off, we were in the parking lot of his apartment complex.

He lived in a plush development, centuries away from my basic square box. I stepped into his contemporary pad. A medium height, black and red lava lamp sat on the coffee table. The dim lighting allowed me to scope the rest of the apartment. African art and carved wooden pieces decorated approximately every other inch of his walls. I felt like I was in an African country with a small campfire during a dedication ceremony. A bit gaudy, but everyone has the freedom of expression. The aroma of strawberry incense filled the room.

Devin closed the door and flicked the light switch on the wall.

I walked slowly toward the black leather couch. A bookcase was on the wall directly opposite the front door. I intended to sit on the couch and casually browse his collection from afar. Gravity took control of my legs and shoved me toward the bookcase. I stood there, boldly, and scanned his library. Feeling eyes burn my back, I turned to face Devin. He was still standing a few steps from the front door, holding his keys in his hand like he was the guest.

"What's wrong?"

His small eyes filled with sincerity. "Nothing. I'm just admiring you."

Pretending that we were at my place, I hospitably said, "Well, relax. Have a seat."

He laughed. "Oh, so you're going to take over in my house, huh?"

With a sleazy wink, I said, "Someone has to take charge."

He winked back. In the light, he was more gorgeous. His denim shorts hung down to his knees. His chest, perfectly swollen, symbolized strength. To avoid stripping naked in the middle of his living room, I immediately turned back to finish my literary analysis.

I asked, "Have you read all of these books?"

"Damn near."

I nodded as to grant my approval, with my lips twisted.

"So, do you read these books for fun or are you an African Studies major?"

He chuckled. "I'm Poli-Sci. I just like to read."

"Really. I wouldn't have pegged you as the Poli-Sci type."

Using his fingers as quotes, he asked, "What is the Poli-Sci type?"

I laughed. "They're usually short and nerdy."

He walked over to me and reached his hand out. My heart sank suddenly. "Now, Ms. Clark, that would be stereotyping. Wouldn't it?"

"No, just observant."

He guided me to the sofa. He slid down on the sofa and put one foot straight out on the coffee table. I sat straight up, a few inches away from him.

"Now that you know a little about me, tell me something special about you."

"Um, I'm from Baltimore. Uh, I'm an Electrical Engineering major—"

He cut me off, "Has anyone ever broke your heart?"

Damn. I was talking. Irritated, I replied, "No."

He sat up and looked into my eyes. "C'mon now. Be honest with me."

As rude as he seemed, his eyes were like sedatives. I calmly blushed. "Honestly." I raised my right hand. "I've never had my heart broken."

He rubbed my arm. "Not necessarily in a relationship, but someone has hurt you."

"The man who killed my father."

I nodded, internal confirmation. How could someone rob a child of the joy of having a father? When I was a kid, I didn't know how much his absence would affect my entire life.

He rubbed my hair. "You wanna tell me about it?"

"Not right now." I immediately jumped to the next subject to avoid exposing my pain. "So, do you like the East Coast so far?"

"I love it."

"Do you plan to stay here when you graduate?"

"I want to go to law school in New York. After that, I'll probably go back to Phoenix and work for my parents."

"Are your parents attorneys or politicians?"

He chuckled. "Attorneys."

"That's alright. They have their own firm?"

"Yep. Patterson and Patterson."

"Wow! So your folks are paid. I guess that explains the car and this upscale apartment." I chuckled softly, relieved that there was a legal explanation for his lavish lifestyle. "Must be nice."

He squirmed. "It definitely has its ups and downs."

Each time he paused between sentences, he had a seductive way of sucking in his bottom lip, and then releasing it slowly to ensure that every crevice was moist.

He continued. "Sometimes I wish I just came from the average lower middle-class family."

"That's easy to say."

He blushed. "Yeah, I know. I sometimes wish that everything wasn't just handed to me."

I hissed. "I wish just one thing was given to me."

He pulled my hand open. "What if I put my heart right there? Would that make you happy?"

I nodded. I forgave myself in advance for breaking my abstinence vow, again. It was only a matter of time before Devin would get it.

Not wanting the night to die, we jumped from topic to topic. His voice had a way of relaxing me. I found myself freely sharing my thoughts. We told childhood stories. We laughed at meaningless jokes. We exchanged energy, emotions, and dreams.

Time ticked away and before we realized it, slits of sun peeped through his miniblinds. I felt closer to him than I had to any other man in my life.

Devin asked, "Do you realize we've been talking for four and a half hours?"

I nodded.

"You want breakfast?"

My stomach barked. I anxiously said, "Sure. Waffle House?"

"Naw, baby. Devin's house."

"Okay. I'm down. What do you have?" I stood to walk in the kitchen.

"I got this." He turned the television on with the remote control and headed toward his bedroom. "Just relax."

Sitting patiently, waiting for a man frightened me. I fumbled with the remote, paged through magazines, and twirled my hair.

Finally, he returned wearing only a pair of gray sweatpants. The waist of his blue polka-dot boxers was visible. Beautiful, dark hair covered his body like satin. I anticipated the day we would lie bare together. The muscles in his stomach formed a washboard. His triceps bulged like he had done a few push-ups while in the room. From the time he appeared in his bedroom doorway, until he made his way to the contemporary kitchen, I stared at him. When he passed me, I noticed an enormous tattoo the size of the *Titanic* on his back. I covered my face with both hands, disgusted by the site. Yuck. I slowly rubbed my eyes. I refocused. The shape of a key lay accurately between his defined shoulder blades. The tip stretched down to the middle of his back. Inside of the head of the key, "KNOWLEDGE" was written in scripted letters in a circular fashion, tracing the outer edge. On the slim part of the key, "IS THE KEY" was written vertically. The soft hair on his back grew inward, appearing to frame the work of art that embellished the deep beige canvas. With such meaning, I was forced to reevaluate his possession of it.

I sat there, watching him maneuver in the kitchen like a chef, wondering what could be his negative qualities.

As the homemade waffles melted in my mouth, I asked, "Who taught you how to cook like this?"

He patted his chest and said, "Can't a brotha just have skills?"

After we ate, he reneged on his promise. He kissed me, slowly, passionately. I was pissed for portraying I was a no-sex-on-the-first-night kind of girl. Isn't the morning after something different? Just as the thought popped into my head, I prayed it out. I didn't want to ruin everything by having sex too soon. I pulled back from his lip lock and looked at my watch. "I need to get home."

He laughed. I smirked. "Honestly."

He nodded and walked out of the kitchen. "Let me get my keys."

I walked into the living room and waited for him at the door. If I stayed one minute longer, I was certain that I would have been stretched across his mattress.

He quickly charted me home. When he pulled up to my apartment, the uncomfortable feeling that I might not talk to him later, never crossed my mind. I was confident that this one was different. I kissed his cheek and stepped out of the car.

When I walked into my apartment, my roommate was still asleep. With my tongue burning to share my story, I called my best friend, Tanisha, in Baltimore. She wakes up with the squirrels. She is the mother of my niece and nephew. My best friend and my brother's babies' mama. Although, she was my best friend first.

Tanisha and I met on the first day of school when I was in third grade. I was moved to a fourth grade class for math. Exceptionally small for my age, I was frightened by the kids. The homely teacher escorted me to an empty desk beside Tanisha. Tanisha squinted her little, almond-shaped eyes like she could read the story of my fear. She pulled the chair out for me and said, "Hi."

Timidly, I sat down and mumbled, "Hi."

Mature beyond her years, she patted my back as to console me. Her deep dimples appeared in the middle of her chubby golden brown cheeks as she offered me a concerned smile.

"You scared?"

I nodded.

"Ain't nuttin' to be scared of, okay?"

From that day on, we were inseparable.

When we reached about thirteen and fourteen, my brother, Reggie, started flirting with Tanisha. When we were younger, he would pinch her fat cheeks just to make her yell at him. Then he started rubbing them slowly with the back of his hand, which always made Tanisha blush. I attempted to ignore the attraction, but it was as clear as Caribbean water.

By the age of fifteen, she presented Reggie with the gift of her virginity. Initially, the relationship was a cute little secret between the three of us. Then it got deeper. Our all-night girl talk ended. When Tanisha stayed over, she would creep into Reggie's room like a thief in the night and return to my room before sunrise. They secretly grew closer and closer. After almost a year of concealing the truth, I was tempted to snitch. Well, just when I was going to tell Mama they were lurking, Tanisha told me she was five months' pregnant. I was forced to shock my mother with a double dilemma. Not only were they a couple, they were having a baby. The news nearly gave my mother a heart attack. Tears streamed from her eyes as she screamed, "You mean to tell me that Reggie been fuckin' Tanisha right under my roof?"

At fourteen, I stood there afraid to answer. "I'on know."

"Clark, don't sit here and tell me you don't know. I know damn well that you know something. Tanisha is like your sister. She's like a daughter to me."

Her eyes pierced through me as I continued to plead my ignorance. "Ma, I'on know."

"This shit is incestuous. How am I 'gon tell people that Reggie done got that girl pregnant?"

I still don't know how she got over the embarrassment, but she did. My niece, Morgan, was born a few months before Reggie departed for college at Duke. After he started school, things fell apart. Tanisha struggled to keep his attention, but he slipped like dress shoes on ice. Somehow, they managed to develop this unique parental bond that I've always envied. As a consequence of their close relationship, Tanisha got knocked up again in her last year of high school.

As much as I love my brother, I despise Tanisha's babies' daddy. It bothers me that he has conquered all of his dreams. He attended Duke on a full academic scholarship. He received an MBA from NYU. He is a successful institutional stockbroker in the Big Apple, while Tanisha's in Baltimore rocking his kids, awaiting his call.

The phone rang twice. Tanisha picked up the phone. "Hello."

I could tell that she was still asleep. I yelled into the receiver, "Tanisha!"

"What the hell is wrong with you, this early in the morning, girl?"

"I met my husband."

Without missing a single detail, I told her about Devin Patterson. She begged for more, but warned, "Clark, be careful. He seems real sweet, almost too good to be true. Don't jump in too deep. You didn't wait this long to give someone a chance to play you. Okay? Call me collect when you give him some."

"You know I will."

"Yeah, I know. Love you."

"Love you, too."

I popped in my En Vogue CD. I got excited each time the chorus would say, "Ooh baby take it, I don't want to tease you."

Apparently offended with my early morning tunes, my room-mate mumbled and staggered around her room. Totally ignoring her frustration, I sang her name. "Erika, can I come in?"

Before she responded, I busted in her room and sat on the bed. I repeated my night once again. With a blasé attitude, she said, "Girl, don't get played. He thinks he's the shit."

I didn't respond. I couldn't respond. Lost for words, I slowly stood and exited her room. I mumbled, "Thanks."

Propped up on a cloud so close to heaven, I could clearly hear the angels singing. I refused to let her get to me.

Lying in my bed, I tossed and turned. Thoughts of Devin danced with anticipation. Finally, I decided to get dressed and go on campus. I put on a black-and-white halter top with a pair of wide-leg black slacks and my black platform slides. I bumper curled my hair. For a last minute do, it flowed down my back like a natural roller set.

When I walked out to my car, there was a note on the wind-shield.

> Clark,
>   I was about to call you to see what time you were going on campus. Just when I was about to pick up the phone, I realized that we hadn't exchanged numbers. If you can, meet me in front of the cafe at 12:30.
> Devin

I glanced at my watch. 12:35. I hopped in my car and drove on campus. After I parked, I walked briskly to the café. When I got there, he was sitting on the steps, tightly grasping a dozen long-stemmed yellow roses.

With a relieved smile, he said, "Hey, sexy lady."

He handed the flowers to me. Tears welled up in my eyes. Everything around me looked blurry, like thick fog had suddenly covered the campus. Jealous stares surrounded me. He stood up when I opened my arms to hug him. I wrapped my arms around his waist and laid my head on his chest.

"Thanks. You didn't have to. I already like you."

*   *   *

After four days without interruption, we reluctantly parted for the first day of classes. When my day was over, I went straight to the apartment to take a nap. Just as I began to doze off, my phone rang.

"Hello."

"Clark . . . baby."

"Hey, Devin. What's up?"

"Can you come over for a while?"

"Sure. Give me about ten minutes."

I jumped in the shower, then threw on a huge Hampton T-shirt that covered my tiny denim shorts. I slipped on my Reebok Princess sneakers and ran out of the apartment.

When I arrived at Devin's place, the smell of chocolate chip cookies seeped through his door. I knocked softly. He opened the door, wearing a pair of cut-off sweatpants. I hugged him. Shower fresh. The hair on his chest softly grazed my face, tickling my curiosity.

He grabbed my arm and walked me into the kitchen. A napkin full of cookies and a tall glass of milk sat on the table.

Delighted by his creativity, I exhaled. "Aw . . ."

He put his hand on my shoulder, massaged it, and motioned for me to sit.

"Devin, what's this all about?"

"I just wanted to do something sweet for you."

I widely stretched my mouth and shook my head. "Devin, you are too special."

He stood behind me and vigorously massaged my neck and shoulders. He gently traced my jawline with his fingertips. I struggled to appear relaxed and eat the cookies, but I wanted him to nourish me. Just when I could no longer bear the craving, I pushed my chair back and stood to face him. We kissed slowly. I forcefully shoved him back to the refrigerator. Sensuously, I tasted his chest and landed moist kisses on his stomach. He appeared to be stunned by my aggression.

He sighed, "Damn, baby."

Desperately, I spoke the words I'd wanted to say since the moment he shook my hand. "Devin, make love to me."

Without hesitation, he placed his hands under my arms and lifted me from my feet. I wrapped my legs around his waist and hugged his neck. I nibbled on his lips as we fervently gazed into each other's eyes. Our hearts kissed and thumped in simultaneous anticipation.

He walked slowly. Eagerly gyrating my body, I moaned. "C'mon, baby. Hurry."

When we got into the bedroom, he laid me down on the bed. He walked over to his armoire and fumbled for a condom. I stripped. When he turned to face me, I was covered with nothing but lust. He climbed over me and delightfully kissed my face. He pushed up against me. I reached my hand down to appraise the precious rock, worthy of possession.

Anxiously, I removed his shorts. As his mouth continued to become acquainted with my body, he skillfully covered the jewel. He rubbed it against me, tantalizing the key to my love. I spread my legs to grant full access. He obliged. He gently buried it deep inside my sacred place. Rhythmic motions. Love. Admiration. Skin bound together by sweat. Pleasurable sighs escaped. Endearing words released. Souls free from despair. Submerged in satisfaction, we lay as one. Lungs searched for confirmation in the air. His heart knocked loudly on my door. I opened.

Atop me, he rose up on his elbows. He stared into my eyes. Softly, he brushed my hair back from my forehead. Affectionately, he landed several sweet kisses on my face.

I nervously spoke his name. "Devin . . ."

Needing him to know, but afraid of scaring him away, I attempted to restrain my emotion, but the words escaped, "I love you."

He laughed quietly and rolled over on his back. Oh, no! My heart sank. How could I be so stupid? He stared aimlessly at the ceiling.

I abruptly rose and sat on the side of the bed. Embarrassed by my vulnerability, I covered my face. After several disheartening seconds passed, he reached up and softly caressed my back.

"Clark, I knew I loved you after the first day. I just thought it was crazy. That's why I'm trippin'. I can't believe you feel the same."

Thankful that the feeling was mutual, I turned to face him. I smiled. "It's not crazy."

"Good, 'cause I love you, too."

I snuggled beside my man. Two lovers on the same track, running the same race.

TWO YEARS LATER

2

CLARK

When I graduated from Hampton, I moved back to Maryland to work for MICROS Systems. The company was in the Howard County suburbs, right outside of Baltimore. I moved into a luxury apartment about ten minutes from work. A temporary stay, because Devin and I planned to move to New York together when he went to law school.

His graduation arrived much sooner than I had anticipated. I was just beginning to master my job when I was forced to start looking for a new job in New York. The thought of leaving my comfort zone made me ill, but the thought of being with my man every day healed the pain.

After sending my resumé to over fifty companies, I hadn't received a response that even insinuated I might get an interview. How could I be completely ignored with my skills? Every company in the Washington Metropolitan area had headhunters blowing up my phone, but no one in New York even dialed my number. Maybe the watermark on the resumé paper said, "Please Don't Call."

Devin suggested I go to New York and stay with my brother, Reggie, for a few days and job hunt. I packed my bags, took a week off, and headed north. I strategically scheduled the trip around the Technical Job Fair in Manhattan.

As I sat on the Amtrak Metro Liner heading to the Big Apple, I imagined all the negative comments I'd hear for the entire week from Reggie. Other than having two kids by a girl whom he doesn't plan to marry, Reggie makes relatively smart decisions.

When the train stopped at Penn Station, I was reluctant to release my bottom from the chair. I climbed the stairs like an old lady with a cane, step by step. It was around six-thirty P.M., right in the midst of rush hour. Thousands of people moved rapidly around me like I was driving thirty mph on the expressway. I walked out to Thirty-second Street, where Reggie normally meets me. After five minutes or so, I spotted the Hunter Green Lexus GS 400.

When he saw me, he pulled the car close to the curb. A cab driver angrily sped around Reggie like he was on his way to deliver a baby.

Finally, he had just enough room to squeeze his car door open. Smiling from ear to ear, he got out and opened his arms. Reluctantly, I stepped in the street and gave my big brother a hug. A little white car zoomed past and practically swiped my bottom off. I jumped. Reggie continued to embrace me despite the angry horns blowing. Though giving hugs was normal, this one was different. It was an explicit sign of sympathy.

With his arms wrapped around me, he backed up to look at his pitiful little sister. "How was the ride, Snook?"

Snook is the nickname he gave me when I was a baby. I can count the number of times on one hand when he has called me Clark. On each of those occasions, he was pretty mad, which only happens once every five years. I answered, "It was okay. I can't complain."

My concerned big brother kissed me on the forehead and finally released me from his bear hug. "You look sleepy."

"I am. I'm ready to go to bed."

He laughed as he grabbed my bags and placed them in the trunk. I climbed in the passenger seat and mentally prepared myself for the lecture. I turned the volume up, so I could practice my ignoring ritual. Surprisingly, he hopped in, still smiling.

"I'm happy you came. You wanna go out tonight?"

The party animal in effect. He can dance for twenty-four hours without taking a break and still make it to work on time. You would think that after fourteen years of partying, he would be tired. He still tries to drag people into the clubs with him. I wasn't in the mood for jumping up and down, which is definitely what he does. I think he's trying to get discovered by a music video producer. He slides all around the floor like a fake Michael Jackson, thinking people are cheering him on. When in reality, they are wondering, "Who is this fool?"

I replied, "Boy . . . I'm looking for a job. I need to get some rest."

"Looking for a job won't be hard. Not with your skills!"

Attempting to ignore his possible sarcasm, I said, "There was a time when it wasn't."

He gave me a sympathetic look. "No calls, huh?"

I shook my head. No need to utter the words.

"Yo, Snook, I can't believe that."

"Believe it."

"Do you think coming up here this week is gonna change that?"

"I hope so."

"Maybe it's a sign."

No comment. I couldn't cry, not so early in the week. Reggie clearly objected to me moving in with Devin. I didn't plan to provide him with any ammunition to support his argument. I turned the music up and pretended his last statement never existed. As we sat in traffic, trying to make a left on Thirty-fourth Street, the anxiety began to take over. Breathe.

People walked in front of the car while the light was green. Cars rested carelessly in the intersection. The light changed three times before Reggie pushed his way through.

When we arrived at his condo on the Upper West Side of Manhattan, I was almost asleep. We drove into the tight little garage. The spaces were so close together that it was impossible not to hit the car next to you. Why people buy nice cars in New York amazes me.

When I walked into the house, I plopped down on his rust leather couch and turned the television on. I noticed a few subtle changes. The pictures on the entertainment center were different. There used to be an 8x10 picture of Tanisha and a 5X7 of Morgan and Little Reggie. A new picture of Morgan replaced the picture of Tanisha.

Reggie put my bag in the second bedroom. When he came out, he danced into the large living room, snapping his fingers. His echo bounced from the ten-foot ceilings.

"Snook, why you so quiet?"

"Didn't I tell you I was sleepy?" I twisted around and propped my head up with the circular suede accent pillow. I rolled my eyes hard like I had just learned the motion was a sign of rebellion.

Reggie grabbed a pillow from the chair across the room and hit me in the head. I popped up and screamed, "Stop!"

He laughed. "Damn, Snook. Why you so touchy?"

The stressful job search robbed me of my childish excitement. I was clearly a grown ass woman, and it didn't feel good. I simply covered my face with the pillow he threw. He got up and went into his bedroom.

"Man, I'm about to roll. You're no fun."

Saddened that he was leaving me alone and upset, I raised up in the chair.

I yelled to the back of the condo, "Where you going?"

No answer. Finally, he walked out of his room with his laptop bag and a backpack. A suit was draped on a hanger in his right hand.

"I'm going over to a friend's house."

As if it weren't obvious, "Who? A female."

Although Tanisha isn't technically his girlfriend, it bothers me that he is a player. His sleeping with Tanisha every time he comes home is probably the bigger issue. He has intentions on marrying Tanisha as much as he plans to quit his 450K per year job at Morgan Stanley Dean Witter and move back to Maryland. Negative. He only sleeps with her because it is easy and disease-free. I definitely believe he loves her, but not the same way she loves him. As long as he gives her an inkling of hope, she won't dare lynch him in child support. Don't get me wrong. Reggie is a damn good father. However, with his salary, the courts would take him to the cleaners. Tanisha would be living lovely, and Reggie wouldn't be driving a Lexus or residing in a plush two-bedroom condo.

Out of curiosity, I asked, "What's her name?"

Without the usual hesitation, he answered, "Sheena."

"She must be real special. Huh?"

Ignoring my sarcasm, he said, "Yep. You'll meet her tomorrow."

Who the hell said I wanted to meet her? Reggie never introduces me to his female friends, willingly. He thinks I'll run and tell Tanisha. This one is apparently different.

"So, is she your girlfriend?"

"You know I don't use that term. But if I did, I guess so."

Looking at him suspiciously, I asked, "Are you in love?"

As I prayed for a negative response, with the most innocent schoolboy grin, he said, "I think so."

Feeling flattered that my brother finally found someone to love, but sad that my best friend could possibly lose the battle, disturbed me. So I asked a stupid question. "Are you coming home tonight?"

"Does it look like I'm coming home?" He raised his shoulders and smiled as he responded to my dumbfounded question. "There's an extra key on the table by the door. I'll get with you tomorrow evening. Call me at work and let me know what time you'll be home. We can grab a bite to eat."

I stood up and gave him a hug. I opened the door. He bent down and kissed me on my forehead.

"Snook, pick your lip up. You're too pretty to be sad."

I nodded and reluctantly smiled. I closed the door and dragged myself into the kids' bedroom like my feet were bricks. I guess *we* included Sheena.

I looked at the meticulous mural of my niece and nephew playing on a playground in the ghetto. No matter how many times I see it, it brings back memories of Reggie and me. I hope they'll have the indisputable sibling love that Reggie and I share. Bright-colored clothing accentuated the brown-toned kids in the background. Hoping that one of the naïve kids in the painting would jump from the double Dutch rope into my body and renew my joyful spirit, I lay patiently on the bottom bunk ready to receive them.

When I woke up the next morning, I dreaded going to the job fair. After I finally got dressed, I felt a tad more inspired. I walked three blocks to the subway station on Broadway and West Eighty-sixth Street. Sharper than a chef's knife, I was prepared to carve into the heart of any recruiter. My navy blue Donna Karan power suit would indubitably assist me. With my hair neatly pulled back into a schoolteacher's bun, I had every intention of going home with offers in hand. After my hike to the station, my pointed Via Spiga shoes that were supposed to mash any doubt into the ground began to crush my corns. In an attempt to alleviate the pain, I leaned from side to side to give each foot a rest.

When I got off the subway two blocks away from the job fair, I felt claustrophobic. Utterly uncomfortable. When I walked into the Sheraton Manhattan Hotel, negative thoughts invaded my mind. My jaws locked shut. Feelings of defeat contaminated me before I approached the first recruiter's booth. How was I supposed to reverse the curse that was plaguing my ambition? After gathering enough courage from the small traces of dust on the floor, I strolled from booth to booth, trying to wheel and deal like a New Yorker. After an hour or so, I left the job fair searching hopelessly for my determination. Where the hell did it go? I walked down to Times Square, looking like a mailman who'd misplaced his bag. People walked swiftly around me, practically shoving me. Bullied by their impatience, I was overwhelmed. They were running on fast-forward, and I was simply on play. New York could never be my home, not even temporarily.

As it got closer to noon, my stomach began to growl. Not to mention, my feet screamed, "Let me outta here!"

I grabbed a huge slice of pizza and headed back to Reggie's place with no desire to find a job in New York.

When I opened the door to Reggie's condo, I wanted to scream. Instead, I climbed in the bed.

When Reggie came home, I heard him slam the door. I intended on lying there as long as I could, to prevent discussing the day's events. I could hear his footsteps on the thickly polished hardwood floor getting closer. He came into the room and woke me up. He looked so lively and happy.

"What's up? Did you find anything?"

Lying, I said, "They're not trying to pay me."

"I guess you're not trying to take a pay-cut. Huh?"

"Hell no!"

"Well, stay in Maryland. That dude ain't worth all the drama you're putting yourself through."

Reggie sounded logical. I sighed and looked him dead in the eye. "Not now."

"So when is the right time to tell you you're being stupid? After you've made a mistake you can't correct?"

I stood up and walked toward the bathroom. "Exactly! I'll be the one correcting the mistake. So let me handle this!"

Realizing that he was fighting a losing battle, he surrendered. "Alright, Snook. You still up for hanging out with me and Sheena tonight?"

Although I didn't want to hear his mouth, it offended me that in the midst of my tribulations, all he could think of was some hoochie named Sheena. He tossed a little advice here and there, but mainly he couldn't give a damn about my life.

When I walked out of the bathroom, I asked, "Why are you so pressed for me to meet her?" I sat down beside him on the bed.

"'Cause I think she's the one."

That stung like a whip on wet, bare skin. Not because I didn't want Reggie to find the one, but because I wondered if I was the one for Devin. He had yet to introduce me to anyone in his family. He made every excuse possible as to why we hadn't intersected after two years. Witnessing Reggie's eagerness for me to meet Sheena made me question Devin's integrity.

Desperately struggling to get my mind off my own relationship, I quizzed Reggie. "So, what are you going to tell Nisha?"

"Nothing. She knows the deal."

I raised one eyebrow and looked at him out of the corner of my eye. "Oh, really?"

Whatever deal Tanisha is supposed to be down with is definitely one-sided.

"Man, you know I love Tanisha. I love the hell out of that girl, but love ain't always the answer. Sometimes you need more than love. We have different interests." He paused like he wished they shared more commonalities. He tightened his lips and looked into the ceiling. He snapped out of his daydream, patted me on my upper thigh, and stood up. "So, don't act silly when you meet Sheena."

How could he confirm to me that Tanisha really wasn't the one? I submitted, "I won't. I still think you need to tell Tanisha something."

"I'm sure you'll handle that."

He walked out of the room. I stormed behind him. "Whatever! I didn't impregnate her . . . twice."

He stopped suddenly. I tripped into him. He turned to face me, his chest swollen, and anger soared from his eyes. Sheepishly, I backed up.

He jiggled his keys. "You going or what?"

I timidly said, "Can I change my clothes?"

He nodded and walked into the living room. He sat there in deep thought. After I rapidly changed into something comfortable, I walked out of the room. He stood up without saying a word. We walked in silence to the garage.

While we were in the car heading to Sheena's apartment, I apologized to Reggie. He softly punched my cheek forgivingly. Almost instantaneously, he began rambling about how much I was going to like Sheena. The more he assured me, the more determined I became not to. How could he expect me to just accept her and automatically think she would be the perfect sister-in-law? His rundown of all of her educational and professional accomplishments made my skin crawl.

We pulled up to a tall apartment building on the Upper East Side. Reggie gave me a get-in-the-back look. I chose not to act rude and did as his eyes commanded. When I opened the passenger door, a tall, slim, light-skinned girl with dreadlocks walked toward the car.

Still holding the door, I ducked my head back in the car. "Is that her?"

Reggie smiled from ear to ear and proudly responded, "Uh-huh."

Definitely not my brother's type. I was tempted to rent a space shuttle to search for the UFO that had abducted my real brother. Reggie dates short, brown women with long hair and big booties. Sheena was the complete opposite. She was extremely beautiful, though. In fact, she was damn beautiful. Her dreads were short and tamed. She wore a dainty denim dress with a pair of black leather Kenneth Cole mules.

When she got in the car, her high-pitched voice sang, "Hey sweetie!"

Before Reggie parted his lips to introduce us, he kissed her. Ugh! I wanted to vomit. My brother, the player, was down for the count.

"Sheena, this is my other baby, Clark. And, Clark, this is Sheena."

Simultaneously we said, "Nice to meet you."

When she turned to greet me, I noticed she had braces. They were her only negative quality. At least I could say something bad about her physical characteristics. She pulled five CDs from her black Prada purse. I laughed softly. Reggie looked in the rearview mirror. "What are you laughing at?"

"Sheena and her CDs."

She turned around with a silly grin. "Girl, I always carry my music."

"I do, too."

"From what Reggie says, we have a lot in common."

Not really wanting to like her, though I already did, I said, "Is that right?"

Sheena could sense my unwillingness to accept her. She didn't respond. She turned to Reggie and started the typical lovers' conversation. They asked each other about their days at work and so on and so on. Then she turned to me. "So, when are you moving here? How's the job search?"

The ghost of reality haunted me again. "Well, I don't exactly have a job. So, I have no idea when I'm moving." I shifted nervously in my seat, preparing to conclude my lie. "I have a few companies interested, but I'll be taking a pay cut. I really don't want to, but I may have to. Money ain't everything."

"I've heard that song before."

She gave Reggie a casual smirk, and they burst into laughter. What the hell was so funny? Reggie, still slightly giggling, said, "Didn't you wish someone told you before you did it?"

Sheena laughed again. "Hell, yeah. I wish I knew then what I know now."

They were having a side conversation and apparently calling me stupid in front of my face. Insecurity tapped softly on my shoulder. Sheena was quickly becoming a name on my shit list.

She turned to face me, removed her Kenneth Cole sunglasses, and set them on top of her dreads. Softly, she said, "Don't mind us. We're being silly."

I looked back at her with my mouth turned to the side and raised my right eyebrow, assuring her that I was unaffected.

She smiled and turned around slowly. Her deeply set almond-shaped eyes concealed wounds, obvious pain residing within. For my brother's sake, I prayed that my analysis was wrong.

Sheena placed the CD in the stereo. Within seconds, "Ascension" by Maxwell blasted from the speakers. Sheena bobbed her head. Pretty down to earth. No wonder Reggie fell in love with her. She has that professional urban swing that Reggie and I treasure so much.

We ate at a cozy spot in Harlem. After a few drinks, we laughed and talked about our childhood like a group of college room-mates. Feelings of betrayal and guilt shook me as I momentarily pictured her as my sister-in-law. We were in stitches laughing at her dramatic interpretations. Reggie seemed to practically crack up like a sitcom audience each time she parted her lips.

After I relaxed, I asked, "What was so funny when you got in the car?" I tried imitating her. "I wish I knew then what I know now."

For the first time all evening, she appeared serious. She reached for my hand and intertwined her fingers in mine. I felt painful energy escaping her palm. She gripped my hand. "Clark, your brother doesn't want you to make the same mistake I made."

"What mistake?"

"Girl, I did the same exact thing that you're about to do. The guy I dated my entire four years in college got a job in Atlanta a few months after graduation. He told me that he needed me there. I left my family. My homies. Took a pay cut. After about six months, that nigga changed. I felt like I was sleeping with a complete stranger. But what could I say? What could I do? I was there alone . . . no friends, no family." She paused as if the baggage was too heavy to carry. "I left home without a promise, without a ring."

With her spirit lifting slightly, she continued, "If this man puts a ring on your finger, by all means, I say pack your shit, but I wouldn't go anywhere without a promise. You have everything to lose."

Refusing to accept Devin would change, I interjected, "Bu—!"

She raised her index finger. "Let me finish. It's not like he dogged me out. It's just that after you get out of school, you grow. Unfortunately, we don't always grow together, at the same rate. And more than anything, he's a man, and men have to see what's out there before they settle down. I know you think he's different, but he's extremely young."

"I know what you're saying, but Devin's not like that. He's very mature."

"Like I said, he's still young. If it's meant to be, you'll withstand the test of time and distance. I really don't suggest leaving your job and your comfort zone to move here. I'm sorry. It's just not a good idea." She smiled gently.

Disputing her view was obviously useless, so I refrained. We pretended the conversation had never occurred and continued to reminisce.

Had I been ignoring all of the warning signs? What if Sheena was right? Maybe Devin did need time and space to grow. If Devin and I did break up, New York was the last place I wanted to live single. Aside from everything, Devin hadn't actually asked for my hand in marriage.

When I woke up, I caught the nine A.M. train back to Baltimore.

3

CLARK

When I got home, I scanned my apartment. My hardwood floors were glistening, mirroring my shadow. I concluded that I was where I needed to be.

After switching the gear in my overnight bag from professional to sporty, I called Devin. No answer. I decided to surprise him. Before I walked out, I cased the joint one last time, absorbing the reality that I was staying.

I hopped into my car and hit the road. The anxiety racing through my veins made the three hour drive feel like thirty minutes. When I saw the sign for Hampton University, my heart sank. I wasn't sure if I should go directly to his apartment or drive around for awhile. I drove on campus looking for Devin, but at the same time hoping to avoid him. Praying he would swallow the news better with some good food, I decided to cook. After I finished cooking, I lay down for a quick nap. The second I slipped into a deep slumber, I heard Devin open the front door. His footsteps made an excited sound pattern like he was rushing to hear good news. That scared the shit out of me.

He sang out my name, "Clark!"

"I'm in the room."

Devin skipped into the room. He climbed on top of me, straddled me, and kissed my forehead. "What are you doing here, girl?"

His affection made me uneasy. I wiggled. "I don't know."

"You don't know. Whassup?" He massaged my upper arms. "Did you get an offer?"

"Well, actually . . . um." What do I say? "Devin, it doesn't look promising."

He relaxed his muscles, his total body weight upon me. Oblivious to my suffering, he spoke, "So what are you saying?"

I pouted my lips, hoping he noticed my desperation. "You know that I really want to move with you to New York, but I can't go without a job."

Still crushing me, he gently swiped my face from forehead to chin with the palm of his hand.

"Yeah, I understand. Stop looking so pitiful. It'll be okay."

"You think?"

"Yeah, it will work out. You don't have to be there by September. You'll definitely find a job within the next year or so. You were only there for a day. You can't give up so easy."

He hopped off of me. Whew! I thought he was going to break my pelvic bone. "Can we eat now?"

Thank God for such a compassionate man. Even though he wanted to object to my decision, he refused to pressure me.

As we ate, a troubled vibe filled the air. My attitude contributed to the feeling. Questions lingered in my head. Just when I was about to break the ice, Devin spoke like he had been masterminding a solution.

"You know, I get enough money monthly to generously take care of the both of us."

Did he actually expect me to put my life and my career on hold? Oh, hell no! That was the last thing I planned to do. I refused to put my entire future solely in his hands. I loved him, but yet I questioned him. As if he never said a word, I switched the topic.

Afraid of the lie about to exit his lips, I nervously asked, "Devin, why haven't I ever met your family?"

He frowned. "I told you."

"Told me what?"

He brushed me off for the fiftieth time. "You'll see them at graduation."

Reggie had almost broken his neck for me to meet Sheena. Surely, if Devin loved me the way he proclaimed, it should be a big thing. Seemingly distracted by my question, he chewed faster. I never imagined the question I've asked a million times could cause so much tension.

Relentlessly, I pressed, "Why have we been together for two years and you don't feel that it's a big thing?"

"It's not."

"Like hell it's not."

Slamming his glass like he could hit me, he stormed from the table. "Look. You'll meet them."

In any other circumstance, I would have fallen for that lame bullshit and calmed down. This time the question meant more to me than ever before. Visions of all the times he'd evaded the question filled my head, I stomped into the bedroom. He lay on his back, with his legs crossed and hands behind his head like my simple question was a complicated equation impossible to solve. I stood at the foot of the bed. Anger rushed to my head and formed wrinkles between my tightly crunched eyebrows. "I'm not special enough for you to introduce me to your family on general purpose?"

I opened my arms. "Why did we have to wait this long?"

In an agitated tone, he asked, "What the hell is wrong with you?"

I demanded, "Yeah, tell me that! What the hell is wrong with me?"

"Clark . . . there's nothing wrong with you. You're trippin'. First, you come here and tell me you aren't moving to New York. Now, you're going off on me about meeting my damn family."

With my neck twisting back and forth rapidly, "Why should I jump up"—I paused—"quit my job"—I paused again. I needed him to understand how stupid the plan sounded. "Move to New York with a man I really don't even know?" I took a long, deep breath. I raised my empty left hand in the air. "And besides, you haven't exactly put a ring on my finger."

He rose up and slid to the edge of the bed. He covered his face with his hands, as if to block me from sight. He slowly eased his hands down his face, simultaneously releasing a sigh of disgust. Disappointment was written all over him. He didn't say a word. He shook his head, slightly letting out a disgruntled snicker every second or so.

As I scrounged for the words to reverse the nightmare into the fantasy that it was when I first walked in the door, I started to pace the floor. Tears rolled down my face. The puppy dog look that would ordinarily get sympathy didn't faze him. He stood up and walked out of the room. I ran behind him. "Devin. I'm sorry."

I grabbed his forearm. He angrily yanked away from me. "Girl, you're trippin'." Gesturing that we were eye to eye, he continued, "I thought we were here."

I followed one step behind. "We are."

He shook his head. "No, we're not."

Trying to place the blame on him, I said, "You're making problems for no reason. I just asked you a question."

He refuted my accusation. "You're the one making the damn problems. I don't need this right now."

In less than one hour, two questions had led him to believe he didn't need this. He didn't need me.

"What are you saying?"

Without hesitation, he repeated his statement. "I don't need the bull shit!"

I begged for his forgiveness. No pity. No reply. He walked back into his room, slammed the door, and locked it. I knocked. I pleaded. He drowned my cries with loud music. Rejection overwhelming me, I bolted from his apartment drenched in agony. What could be a reasonable excuse for his reluctance to introduce me to his family?

4

DEVIN

Clark wept outside my bedroom door. I wanted her to stay there and think about her accusations. I needed her to realize that temper tantrums aren't effective with real men.

She sniffled, "Devin, I love you. Please open the door."

It hurt me to hear her cry. I felt her desperation, but I refused to submit.

She tapped softly. "I'm so sorry."

Just as my hormones were singing rejoicing melodies because I could finally indulge in my smooth chocolate on a daily basis, she wasps in to say she wasn't moving to New York.

She begged, "Devin, I need you."

Just like she needed whatever was stopping her from being in New York. I tried to block out her voice. My skin crawled as she repeated, "Devin, I love you. I want to be with you."

I slid under my quilt and covered my head. Childishly, I placed my hands over my ears and began to hum. I thought of my family. The people I've protected Clark from. Their judgments. Their convictions. Their scrutiny.

With each breath Clark took, I heard my mother's voice scorn me, "Devin, don't get hooked up with any of those fast girls at that little college."

Hampton wasn't her school of choice for me. My parents, Stanford alumni, felt Hampton was a smack in the face. Her voice rang louder as Clark cried harder, "They'll only hold you back. An Ivy League school is different. The girls there are different. They are going where you're going. They're not looking for a handout."

Neither was Clark, but how was I to explain to my parents that my six-thousand-dollar-a-month allowance wasn't why Clark loved me so much. I couldn't. So, I didn't.

5

CLARK

I stumbled into my apartment after my long, tearful drive from Hampton. In my empty queen-sized bed, I cried myself to sleep. My life was in shambles.

When I woke up, my head pounded like someone hit me with a hammer. I checked my messages. Both my mother and Tanisha left several messages. I laughed at their silly ramblings. After hearing their voices, I knew I was going to Mama's house. Waiting in the apartment alone, hoping he'd at least call to see if I arrived safely, would kill me.

I called my mother. She picked up the phone sounding lively. "Praise God!"

"Mommy . . ." At the age of twenty-four, I still managed to whine.

"Girl, I have been worried about you. You ain't called nobody."

"I know, Mommy. When I got back, I went straight to see Devin."

"Clark, I never thought I'd see the day that you would run after a man like you do."

My mother is the one who taught me how to protect my heart. With Devin, I couldn't find the strength. He swept me off my feet. Mama's philosophies disappeared in the midst of the dust. Discarding all of her relationship lectures like bad habits, I fell for all of Devin's tricks.

I pretended to be the happy young lover. "Well, Mama, when it's good, it's good." I lied. "Anyway, I am off for the rest of the week. You want some company?"

"Yeah, sweetie. I'm surprised you ain't stay with Devin."

"I know. I'll be there in a few."

"Drive safely."

I grabbed my bag again and left my junky apartment. I chanted softly to myself, "On the road again."

When I arrived in Baltimore, I stopped at Tanisha's job, Hair Etc. When I walked in the door, everyone turned to face me like I was wearing bells. Tanisha smiled. "Hey, Boo!"

I sluggishly called back, "Hey, girl!"

Luckily her station is the second one after passing the receptionist's desk. I hate walking past the other stylists, because they look at you like hungry lions. They make you feel like you are planning a robbery, which always killed my desire to patronize the place. Tanisha is the sweetest one in the shop, which is probably why her clientele booms the way it does. Not to mention, the girl has skills when it comes to hair. You would think she was giving away free cheese on Fridays and Saturdays. The other stylists, as well as their regular clients, always concentrate more on the etcetera and less on the hair. Everyone's business is public stock in Hair Etc.

I gave Tanisha a big hug and mumbled, "Uh, uh, uh."

As she stuck the curlers back in the stove and sipped her soda, she asked, "What's wrong?"

Her comment caught the attention of the client sitting in her chair, as she awkwardly turned around to see my expression. Thankfully, all the other beauticians were into *The Young and the Restless.* I proceeded to whisper the details of what happened at Devin's house. Tanisha shook her head. She attempted to conceal her genuine emotion when she looked at me.

"Girl, you're crazy. But I know what you are saying, though. Plus, I don't want you all the way up there anyway."

She laughed as she evidently imagined me being in New York. "Hell, if you move up there. I'll just pack my bags. Act like the crazy Baby Mama and move in with Reggie."

Uh-oh! Sheena had slipped my mind. Her attempt to make me laugh backfired. Every line in my face insinuated that I was withholding valuable information. Visions of Sheena and Reggie's lovers' glow filled my mind. I looked around the salon for the words to tell my best friend that I wasn't the only one with shattered dreams.

"Trick!" I jumped. She'd obviously called my name several times. "Why are you in a daze?"

Trying to appear cool, "Why wouldn't I be?"

"I guess you're right."

The second she said that, the door opened and relieved me of the mundane duty to tell my friend what was really bothering me. It was one of Tanisha's customers.

She greeted her, "Hey, Boo. Let Kelly wash your hair."

Tanisha construed my expression like words on paper. She finished styling the lady in her chair. Then she respectfully told her other clients that she was going outside to eat her sandwich. Damn. The perfect words simply vanished from my brain.

She grabbed her food and headed toward the door. I stood motionless. As she turned her five-foot frame around, her black smock with her face airbrushed on the front swung in my direction like a graceful church fan. "Are you coming?"

When you love someone like I love Tanisha, it's hard to camouflage things you know you're obligated to tell. I walked toward the door like a shy toddler, turned, and said my good-byes to the other stylists, which I never do. Bad sign. Tanisha held the door with her foot stretched behind her. She turned her head around. "C'mon. I don't have long."

Tanisha knows I don't like to get explicit in the shop, because eyes and ears lurk like sharks. They will always come back to bite and chew you to mortality.

She opened the passenger door of my car and sat inside. As I walked around to the driver's side, I attempted to gather the courage. Was there really any way to make it less painful?

Unfortunately the truth hurts just like needles, but they both provide pathways to the cure. Tanisha peeled the foil from her food and took a bite. As she chewed, she wiped the side of her mouth with a napkin.

"Now, how the hell did you go to New York and let that jerk, Reggie, change your mind like that."

Slowly, I began, "Well, I prayed and . . ."

"And . . ."

"And after no one paid me any attention at the job fair, I said forget it."

"You're giving up that easy."

After the cold way Devin had treated me, I was content with my decision. "Now it is."

She nodded. "I know that's real."

I drifted slowly on to another topic. As I rambled about nothing, Tanisha skipped on to talk about her love. "Reggie told me y'all had a nice time."

Reluctant to speak of the two-timer, I said, "Did he?"

She swallowed the food in her mouth. "Yep. He called the shop yesterday after he dropped you off."

Trying to determine just how much information he'd shared, I asked, "Really. What did he say?"

"Nothing much. Just that y'all went to dinner."

Nothing about Sheena, huh? "Did he tell you who we went to dinner with?"

"Yeah, Sheena." It flowed out so naturally, with such lack of concern.

Baffled. "You know her?"

"I met her when I took Morgan up there last summer. She works with Reggie. I used to talk to her when I called the office. I think she has her own group now. I haven't talked to her in a while."

Puzzled that she'd kept this from me, "Why didn't you tell me about her?"

Oblivious to the nature of Reggie and Sheena's relationship, she brushed it off. "I don't know. It wasn't a big issue."

My mouth opened wide enough to fit in a basketball. "She *is* a big issue."

Confusion covered her round face. "What are you talking about?"

"She and Reggie are a couple." I stressed, "Caught up!"

Damn. It came out too harsh. I would have given someone a

million bucks to retrieve the words that had parted my lips. Too late. She absorbed them. Her eyes turned red like she'd just swallowed a shot of Absolut vodka.

"Clark, don't play with me. I will kill him."

I raised my arms. "That's what they told me. What did you think they were doing?"

"Clark, when I met that whore, she talked me to death about her ex-boyfriend. I thought they were just buddies." Her voice weakened. "He claimed that she reminded him of you."

Just to think I even liked the shady whore. She continued to replay all the instances Reggie had pretended nothing was going on. "You mean that bitch smiled in my face for an entire four days and was sleeping with my man?"

How could Sheena fraudulently act as a mere home-girl for Tanisha? My only guess was that Reggie was the only one caught up.

"Nisha, I'm sorry. I didn't know."

She looked at me, attempting to cover the scars of betrayal that were growing a tumor in her heart. "Clark, you didn't know. You don't have to apologize. You're my girl no matter what. Like you always say, 'we're in a sticky situation.'"

"That, we are."

She wiped the thin tracks of tears from her face with the tip of her index finger. "I have to come get the kids when I get off, so I'll see you at Mama's."

She jumped out of the car and left her sandwich lying in the passenger seat. The meaty steak and cheese looked like saltine crackers to me. My stress filled me to capacity, and Tanisha obviously felt the same.

Angry that Reggie hadn't given me the 411 before I ran my mouth, I rushed to my mother's house. I should have let that bastard tell her himself. I felt grungy for spilling mud on my girl's clean conscience.

I called Reggie the moment I walked in the door. He shouted, "Why the hell are you so stupid?"

"Stupid? You didn't tell me that Tanisha met her."

"I didn't have to."

Guys are *real* assholes. That was a crucial piece of information. Tanisha had heard about and accepted other women before. The reason she was devastated was because she felt betrayed. Not only by Reggie, but some hooker that she actually grew to like.

"Dummy, she's so mad because she thought you two were just friends!"

"No, she's mad because I have to let her go."

He continued, "I'm mad that you would tell her while she was at work. I knew you was 'gon tell her, but at work. Damn, Snook. That was real stupid! You know how those girls in that shop talk."

Feeling worse than before, "I guess you're right. I'on know what I was thinking."

"You weren't!"

"Look, don't make me out to be the bad person here."

"I'm sorry, Snook. For real, though, when Nisha met Sheena, we *were* just friends." He took a deep breath. "We just made it official about two months ago. Man, we were like boys, and one day I realized I loved her."

He paused, waiting for a compassionate response. During the same time, he was still laying up with my girl. Whatever.

"It just felt right. I woke up and I knew she was the one."

As the reality of his words traveled through my veins, I felt my brother's sincerity. It seemed shady, but I sympathized with him. I believed him.

"I can come home and talk to Tanisha face-to-face, if you think she might handle it better that way."

No. Actually I didn't think she needed or wanted to see him. "Reggie, you've done enough already."

"Snook, don't trip on me like that. Tanisha's my baby. I don't want to see her hurt either."

"I understand, but I think she needs her peace right now. You coming here will only send her the wrong sign."

"Alright, Snook. I gotta go. Give her a kiss for me and tell her I'm sorry."

I slammed the phone down without mumbling a sound. Why is it men think they can rip your heart into shreds and you want their kisses? To hell with his kiss!

Mama made my favorite meal. Crab cakes and potato salad. Her spicy southern food is always the perfect remedy for a broken heart. Once the smoke cleared, I was finally able to tell her about Devin.

I thought she would scorn me for being so needy. Instead she said, "Clark, no man likes to be questioned or second-guessed. You wouldn't like it. As far as his parents go, I don't think it's as serious as you make it sound. I think he just hasn't found the right time. From what you say, they are busy people. I wonder if they even have time to see him, nonetheless his girlfriend. How many times has Devin gone home since you've known him?"

"About three times."

"Alright, then. It sounds like he doesn't deal with them himself. Why would he want you to meet them? As for marriage, Clark, you're still young. Since you've known him, y'all said after law school. The boy ain't even outta Hampton yet, and you're already acting crazy. You can't have everything at once. Didn't I teach you that?"

I was tripping. Though I'd forgiven him, I decided to let him sweat it out for another night, because he needed a lesson in the way to treat Clark. He *should* have noticed that I was stressed. He *should* have held me. He *should* have whispered positive words in my ear. No, instead he flipped out.

When Tanisha finally walked into the house, the kids ran to her screaming, "Mommy!"

When she grabbed Morgan, she started crying. Unaware of why, Morgan cried, too. Then I started crying. Gathered in a group hug, we all cried. I cried because I understood Tanisha. I also cried because I didn't understand Devin. My life was falling apart like rusted paint, one chip at a time.

Through spit bubbles lining her full lips, Tanisha said, "He said he loves her."

I hugged her again, because I had no words to console her. Through the pain that shined so vividly on Tanisha's face, it was obvious Reggie was living two lives. My girl was covered with emotional scars inflicted by my brother. Talk about domestic violence.

Tanisha fumbled around the house. She walked into the kitchen.

My mother opened her arms. She lay limp on my mother's shoulder. "Mommy, it just hurts so bad."

My mother rubbed her back. "Baby, don't you worry 'bout nobody. I know my son, and he loves you and only you."

I stood in the doorway, wondering why my mother would give her a reason to hold on. Just as she knows her son, I know my brother. Reggie loved Sheena. His heart was all tied up, and I was afraid that Tanisha wouldn't be able to loosen the knot.

My eyes pierced through my mother's sympathy. I slowly shook my head. She noticed my sign. "He loves you, but if he can hurt you like this, you gotta let go."

I smirked, approving of my mother's advice. Tanisha let go. "Mommy, I know. I'm going to let him go. I'm just scared."

Tanisha grabbed Morgan's backpack from the kitchen counter. "Come on, Clark, walk me to the car."

Just as we got to the car, she stared at me like she saw Reggie all over me. "My best still wasn't good enough, huh?"

Witnessing her anguish frightened me. She'd loved this man, only him, her entire life. What a terrible payback. What if I waited? Where would I end up?

I wrapped her in my arms, hoping to squeeze all the self-doubt from her. "Nisha, Reggie is just selfish. He has always been that way."

She nodded. I continued, "You are too good for him."

She nodded again, but she didn't want to believe a word I was saying. Still, I tried to convince her. "He doesn't deserve you. He has never deserved you."

Her chest rose and fell rapidly. Though true, my words were not making her feel any better. She reached for the door handle. I patted her back. "It's going to be okay."

She sat in the car. I sniffed back my tears. "Call me if you need me."

She nodded and started the car.

I rushed into the house to check my voice mail. No messages. If not to apologize, he could have at least checked to see if I was killed on the highway. Nothing.

When Tanisha dropped the kids off the next morning, she

came in with no evidence of pain. Never had I been so excited to see Tanisha's dimples.

"All better."

"Yep. All cried out."

"Really."

"Girl, you know after I cry it out, I'm good."

"Are you up for going out Friday?"

"Hell, yeah!"

Before I went out, I checked my messages one last time. Nope, not even a simple hello. I put on some skin-tight jeans, a black Planet Hollywood (Paris) T-shirt, and black leather boots. I pulled my hair up into a spiky ponytail. As we looked in the mirror, at our Glamour Girl faces, we were positive that we could generate enough energy to have any man follow us like a dog in heat.

We went to Larry Stewart's Place, a cozy spot where you cross all kinds of Black folk. Whatever floats your boat, it was sure to be found at Larry's.

When we walked in, the jazz band was playing, "She's a Brick House." Eyes drilled holes in our clothes as we strutted rhythmically to the tune like supermodels. We walked up the steps to get a table in the lounge.

We sat at a table for two and discussed the dramas, in which we were the lead actresses. After about ten minutes, a little Mexican guy with dusty green pants and an ashy black T-shirt came over to the table.

"A rose for the pretty ladies." He handed both Tanisha and me a rose.

Okay, that was cute. After the tenth time, we told him not to come back. Our small square table was buried under red roses. We summoned the extra-slim waiter. He hustled over. He folded his arms and pretended to whisper as he spoke with a feminine lisp. "You see that guy over dere."

With a bunch of guys in the direction his head was pointed, we giggled. "Which one?"

He rolled his eyes and blushed. "That big fine one with the Nike T-shirt and the black cap."

We nodded. He continued, "He the one"—he pursed his lips and blinked—"that's been sending the roses, and he said get what y'all want, 'cause he got the tab."

Tanisha smiled at the nice-looking guy approximately in his mid-thirties. He winked. She waved to him. When he walked to the table, Tanisha flirted.

"So, Mr. Big Guy. What's your name?"

He reached out his thick arm and shook Tanisha's hand. "I'm Fred Wilkins."

Tanisha smirked. "Would that be the Fred Wilkins who owns Daring Hair I and II?"

Oh, no! Drug dealer. I shouldn't be so cynical, but most hustlers own salons in Baltimore. He blushed. "That's me. The one and only."

Still gripping his hand, "Well, I'm Tanisha from Hair Etc."

"You gotta be kidding. Nobody ever told me you looked like Lela Rochon. I would have come to find you a long time ago."

Flattered by his compliment, Tanisha giggled. "Well, now you can see with your own eyes."

He completely ignored my existence. I stood up. "Here, you can take my seat."

Realizing his ignorance, he said, "Oh, I'm sorry. Fred."

"It's okay. I'm Clark. Nice to meet you."

Tanisha cosigned. "Yeah, that's my girl, Clark."

"I'll be downstairs."

Tanisha waved at me without hesitation. She was eager to have a conversation with this Fred Wilkins.

I sashayed down the steps with pizzazz. By the time I reached the bottom step, men were recruiting me from all sections of the bar, but my attention was on the only guy not sweating me. His bald head gave light to the dimly lit bar. Arrogance surrounded him. I gravitated to him like a hurricane. I walked straight in front of the chest of steel and asked, "Can I buy you a drink?"

He bent down slightly to answer me. A huge diamond stud lurking on his earlobe glistened like it was recently dipped in jewelry cleaner.

"Naw, sweetheart, my daddy ain't raise me like that. Can I buy *you* a drink?"

His sexy southern drawl soaked my panties.

"No, I'm fine for now. Let's get a table."

"Can I get your name, miss?"

"That would be Clark. And your name would be?"

"Take a guess."

I was not in the mood to play the name game. "Never mind. I'll find someone else to come upstairs with me."

I turned to walk away. He grabbed my hand. "Slow down, Feisty Lady. I'm RJ. I just thought you recognized me."

Why would I? "I'm not good with names. And where should I know you from?"

He bashfully said, "Nowhere. I shouldn't assume."

"I guess. Are you ready to go upstairs?"

"Yeah." He grabbed his drink from the bar and followed me.

Tanisha winked at me from across the room, approving of my catch. She and Fred looked like two birds alone in the wilderness singing tunes.

RJ and I sat at a table near the bar. The moment we sat down, a waiter came to shake his hand. "Good season, man."

RJ brushed him off. "Thanks, man."

He pushed his hand up against mine. "You have large hands to be such a little lady."

"You know what they say about ladies with big hands."

"No, what's that?"

"Just joking. I don't know."

We both laughed.

"Clark, you are sexy as hell."

We were interrupted again by a couple walking out. The guy said, "Man, you had a hell of a season."

Again RJ humbly said, "Thanks, man."

He stood to shake the guy's hand and patted him on the back. "C'mon, baby. Let's go in the back."

I followed him to the back of the lounge. "You must be a popular guy."

When we finally sat down, he began to rub my hands again. "Clark, I play for the Ravens."

"Yeah, I figured you were an athlete. I just didn't know which sport."

He smiled. "I like you, gurl."

Uncertain of what I wanted from him, I said, "Is that right?"

"Yeah, I could spoil you, gurl."

Again, "Is that right?"

"Yep. I could love you all night long."

Something about him aroused me. "Really."

"Candles. Jazz. Ice. Strawberries. Whip cream."

Why was he turning me on so? In ten minutes, I'd concluded that I wanted to have a one-night stand with RJ.

He continued, "I'll pour hot wax all over you. Just when you can't take it anymore . . ."

He paused. Anxiously awaiting the finale to his pornographic narration, I leaned in closer. Taking seductive breaths, he continued, "I'll take ice from the bucket and rub it all over you. Then I'll put the ice inside of you."

He motioned his fingers like he was performing the insertion. I wiggled nervously in my seat. My eyes full of desire, I stared into his.

"Slowly, I'll put myself in." Hypnotized by his vivid description, I took a soft breath. He started laughing. "Gurl, let me stop. I'll have you sprung."

Devin who? "It's okay. I've got some tricks in my bag, too."

"Gurl, you're something else. Like what?"

Gulping the last of my drink, my bad girl twin said, "I can show you better than I can tell you."

"That's what I'm talkin' 'bout, a lady in touch with her sexuality."

I laughed. More like a woman scorned. Devin would have to beg for another piece of his pie.

"So, you ready to get out of here or what?"

My heart sank. "RJ, I need to run to the rest room. I'll be ready when I get back."

When I stood, I summoned Tanisha. The second we got into the small bathroom, I said, "Nish, I'm gonna fuck that dude."

I waited for her lecture. She giggled. "I know that's real, girl. I might fuck Fred, too."

What? My role model wanted to have a one-night stand. How could she succumb to such a temptation? She doesn't even kiss men until after a month or two.

"Tanisha, no!"

She shook her head. "I'm tired of living for Reggie . . . it's time to get my freak on."

She twirled her wide-set hips and gave me a high-five. The words were perverted coming from Tanisha's mouth. All I could do was hand her two condoms from my purse. "Strap up."

The consummate mother said, "You, too, but I need to get his tag number and name."

"Tanisha, please?"

"You know I don't play."

We walked over to RJ together. I introduced them.

Tanisha looked at me like I was a lunatic. "What is his *real* name?"

I raised my shoulders and looked at RJ. "I'on know."

RJ reached out to shake Tanisha's hand. "Rubenstein Hamlet, tight-end, Baltimore Ravens."

Tanisha smiled. "Thank you. Now all I need is your tag number."

"No problem. Y'all ready?"

We all walked out together. Fred seemed nice, but I thought he was a bit flashy, definitely on the wrong side of the law.

We got inside of RJ's silver Toyota Land Cruiser. Our conversation immediately switched gears. He got intellectual on me. He kept saying, "I go for you, gurl."

When we arrived at his home in Owings Mills, we were in the sack in a matter of minutes. I lay in another man's quarters, serving him all of Devin's dessert. Drip. Drop. RJ licked the saucer as not to leave a crumb behind. While I provided pleasure for another man, Devin's spirit circumvented me and immobilized my body. Why hadn't he called? What would he think if he knew I was there?

When I woke up, I was ready to leave. He wanted to eat breakfast. I was disgusted as if he had forced me to go to his home. I wanted to get away from him, fast. The attractive man I saw through drunken eyes now looked like a drooling bulldog. During the ride, he rambled on about how he wanted to stay in contact. I ignored the hell out of him and prayed that he would just shut up. By the time we got to my mother's house, I wanted to jump out of the moving truck. I took his number out of courtesy, didn't offer mine, and promised I'd call. I lied.

When I walked into my apartment after four days, the smell of Pine-Sol filled the air. For a second, it slipped my mind that I hadn't cleaned the place before I left. I walked into my bedroom. The clothes that I left scattered around the floor were hung neatly in my closet. Devin!

I stood there overwhelmed, searching within for an explanation for my actions. I should have known Devin wouldn't leave me out there. Why did I sell us short? How could I be so spontaneous with our body? There was a note on my bed. He wrote:

> Baby,
>   I'm so sorry for trippin' the other day. I just have a lot on my mind. Bear with me. Page me when you get in.
>
> Devin
>
> PS. I see you made it back.

My body was numb. It never even dawned on me that he would be at my place. I paged him. Within thirty minutes, there was a knock at the door. Before I could get there, Devin put his key in the door and walked in. When I looked at him, guilt swirled in my stomach like warm milk. Afraid that my face vividly displayed photos of last night, I wanted to regurgitate my indiscretions.

He walked over to me and held me tightly. The warmth generating in his arms let me know that he'd do anything to prevent me from slipping away. No words were mumbled, but forgiveness escaped our hearts and understanding was discovered. We spent the entire day together. I prayed that he'd be ready to head back to school after dinner. Wrong! He came back to the apartment to get a small serving of dessert. Think quickly.

I walked into the bathroom. I repeatedly pushed my finger down my throat. Suddenly the sin inside of me came thrusting out. I dramatically kneeled on the floor and embraced the toilet bowl as I continued to gag. Devin ran in. "Are you okay?"

I wiped my filthy mouth and nodded. He stooped down and wiped the tears that rolled from my watery eyes. "You want me to get you some Coke or something,"

"Yeah."

With such concern, he rushed into the kitchen. I stood to brush my teeth. I gloated in the mirror. My self-imposed nausea provided the perfect excuse for not being in the mood for sex. Being a player is like riding a bike; you never forget.

6

CLARK

It seemed like I was on vacation for only a weekend. I planned to get in early so I could enjoy the rest of my evening shopping in Georgetown. In less than a week, my life's plans had changed drastically. There was no longer a clear understanding of what my future held. I turned up the radio to listen to Russ Parr and Olivia Fox, hoping to get a laugh before I faced reality. I had to conjure up the words to tastefully kiss ass as I explained to my manager that I wouldn't be resigning from MICROS Systems.

Mike, my manager, is a tall, arrogant white man. For some reason, I have him wrapped around my finger. He agreed with all my suggestions, promoted me when I did and didn't deserve it. A lot of folks in our division think he has jungle fever, but I don't complain. I poke my chest out, smile real pretty, and kindly accept all of my equal opportunity bonuses.

When I told Mike I planned to move to New York, he acted as if the entire division would collapse without me. He offered more money, more control. I declined and assured him my mind could not be changed.

I drove into the parking lot on Columbia Gateway Drive. Full of dread, I stepped out of my car. My brain motioned like an eternal Ferris wheel. Walking into his office and discarding my armor of pride petrified me. I had to pretend I'd simply decided it would be best to stay. Two weeks prior, nothing could keep me. Now, I ironically had come to my senses. Mike had been interviewing people for my position. Surely he'd found someone. Where would that leave me?

I slowly walked toward the building with my head hung low like a slave in chains hoping the "good massa" would be kind enough to let me stay on the plantation. I was dressed like a diva on Sunset Blvd., sunshades covering my doubtful expression. An unsuccessful job search had damaged my self-esteem like an abusive relationship. I questioned everything about me, my relationship with Devin, my move to New York.

When I walked into the office, everyone wanted to talk.

"Clark. How was New York?"

"Fine," I mumbled.

I stared at the floor until I reached my desk, hoping to avoid small talk with my coworkers. They all wanted to know about my job search. Like a fool, my big mouth had told the entire office about my plans to relocate. My inability to find a job would confirm their suspicions. They would think I'd been Mike's little token all along. The smart little black girl who rose at the speed of lightning at MICROS wasn't capable of getting an interview in the Big City.

Before I could put my empty briefcase down, Mike came over to my cubicle. "Clark, I need to see you as soon as you get settled." As he turned to walk away, he chuckled a little. "Oh, how was New York?"

What was so funny? Was desperation written on my face?

"I'll be there in a minute."

Hell. Why me? What does he want? What if he wanted a final date of resignation? Had he found someone to take my position?

After taking what seemed like fifty deep breaths, I walked toward Mike's office, dreading each step like I was walking into a ring of burning flames. Attempting to appear poised, I fixed my clothes.

As I entered his office, he motioned for me to close the door while he wrapped up his daily morning conversation with his wife.

"Clark, Clark, Clark . . ."

I folded my arms, trying to conceal the throbbing beat under my suit jacket. With a half smile, I retorted, "Mike, Mike, Mike . . ."

"Are you definitely leaving us?"

Unsure of the booby trap that was being designed, I asked, "Why?"

"Well, we want to make you an offer that you can't refuse."

Whew! I wiped my forehead with the back of my hand, hoping to erase any evidence of neediness. My confidence appeared from its hiding place like a mouse realizing everyone left the house.

"Really."

"Really. Well, while you were away, we ran into a few problems."

"And?"

"Everyone was clueless. I talked to higher management to see what we could do to make you stay. I made it absolutely clear to them that you would need something to literally sweep you off your feet." Jokingly, he continued, "I know it has to blow you away to compete with that hunk Devin.

"Considering that the problem is still up in the air, we are desperate. I guess we will have to pay for it, though. It's mainly my fault, because I haven't been preparing for your departure. I know you are sharp, but I didn't realize that you are a one-man team until last week."

Certainly perplexed, but whatever they were offering, I was accepting. Refusing to show, in any way, that I had to stay, I nodded.

Mike cleared his throat, removed his glasses. He leaned back in his high-back, mahogany leather chair and placed his hands behind his head.

"I've been interviewing for other positions in the company. And I recently accepted one. With so much concentration on my career, I've let some things around here slip. It became adamantly clear to me last week that I could not leave this division in this shape."

He paused. "You are the glue that keeps this place in order. If you leave, I can't possibly pursue my personal career objectives."

He sat upright. "What I'm saying is will you take my position?"

Before I could part my lips, he cut me off. "Fifty percent more than your current salary."

I wanted to jump up and down and scream, "Hell, yeah!!" but I refrained.

"Mike, you know this is a lot to take in. I have to speak to Devin before I make a decision."

"How do you feel about it? Is the money enough to make you at least consider staying?"

With a confident smirk, I said, "We'll see. I'll have to talk to Devin. Okay?" I stood, obviously assuming our conversation was done.

"Just a second. That's not it."

I slid back into the chair.

"The problem that I told you about when we first started talking."

I nodded.

"Well, it's a big problem. Monstrous."

"Mike, you know I hate when you beat around the bush."

"I know, but I am laying so much on you at once. I feel bad."

"Don't."

"Well, Les Flam's." He paused. "The chain in France." He waited for a reaction. "They are having major problems with the systems. It appears to be a virus, maybe. The systems won't accept credit card payments."

"Yeah . . . so." I motioned for him to continue.

"Well, we need someone there, at their site."

Taken aback by the thought, I blurted, "You want me to go to France?"

"Yes. You are the only one I trust, not to mention the only one that my superiors trust. Even if you don't stay with the company, could you please help us solve this problem?"

Certain that I was staying with the company, I decided to gather the details. "When do you need me in France? And for how long?"

Shaking his head and nervously smiling, he said, "As soon as possible, and until the problem is solved. They are losing money daily."

"No one else has a clue?"

"No one."

"I could be there for weeks." As the words flowed from my mouth, I remembered Devin's graduation.

"Clark, we plan to do whatever you need to accommodate you."

Appearing to be distraught, I took a deep breath, closed my eyes like I couldn't handle eating everything that was placed on my plate. "Mike, Devin graduates in two weeks. I can't miss it. I don't know."

"Clark, I will guarantee you a huge Performance Award when you return, aside from the ten percent bonus. We're begging."

"I need to think. I'll give you a definite answer after lunch."

He apprehensively nodded.

As I turned the doorknob, Mike said, "Clark, the ball is in your court. Ask for whatever you want." He winked. "You can get it."

"Thanks, Mike." I like that about him. He always lets me know how to go farther and get the most for my skills. If nothing, I owe it to him to go to France. He has supported everything I've done in my few years with the company. He is the reason for my success.

When I phoned Devin, it was an informative conversation, because there was nothing to consider. I had to go to France, because I had to keep my job. It was that simple. Not to mention, they were throwing money at me like I was running for president.

As I rambled on nervously, Devin interrupted me. "Clark, I understand. You can't change what you have to do." He snickered slightly. "You sound like you were scared to tell me."

"I was scared to disappoint you."

"Baby, graduation is a long, boring ceremony. It's okay if you don't make it. You have been there when I needed you. You helped me get here. That's all that matters."

"You sure?"

"Yeah, I'm sure. I'm coming back to see you when I get out of class. I'll be there by the time you get off."

"Really?"

"You know I can't let you go to France, indefinitely, without seeing you."

Considering the doubt that had so recently reared its ugly head in our relationship, I wasn't so sure. "I'll see you when I get home, okay?"

"Later."

After lunch, I walked into Mike's office. With a humble attitude, I told him that I would accept his proposal.

"So, when do I leave for France?"

"The earliest you can get a flight is Wednesday. Is that good for you?"

"Yes. I can do Wednesday. When will I be taking over the branch?" Trying to cover up my abrupt arrogance, I said, "I mean, when are you accepting your new position?"

"I'm looking at four weeks from today. Hopefully you'll be back by then."

Hopefully? I planned on being back in two weeks.

"Yeah, I'll be back by then."

Devin hadn't arrived when I got home. I cracked a can of Bud Ice in my refrigerator, changed into my gray sweats, and lit my frankincense. I lay diagonally across my bed, staring out of the window, hoping to absorb some wisdom from the mature sun staring through the panes. Just as my calming ritual began to relax my anxious mind, I heard Devin.

I walked into the hall to greet my honorable prince. Without mumbling one word, I hugged him. Our bodies were like metal being melded together by a flame. He ran his fingers upward through my hair, making a ponytail by grasping my entire mane in his hands. He tilted my head back, bent down, and absorbed every taste in my mouth. I lifted his T-shirt and put my bare palms on his sculptured chest, trying to feel the vibration of true love that used to reside in his temple. As I gently rubbed his torso, he bent down and placed his head under my shirt. He moistly decorated kisses on my stomach, while simultaneously pulling down my sweatpants, discovering the bare beauty. I slowly raked his back. He guided his hands down to the backs of my thighs, massaging each with vigorous strokes. Then he proceeded to send his fingers on a search for the treasure that we both claim. He softly brushed back and forth to force the release of wetness from the warm surface. He grabbed my legs and picked me up as he rose to his feet. In silence, we stared intensely into each other's eyes as he carried me into the bedroom. He laid me on the bed, then stood at the bottom, discarding his clothing. Wanting me to beg, he remained there, naked, wholly aroused for an eternity.

Uttering the first words since he entered the apartment, I begged, "Come on, baby."

Without further delay, he submerged passionately into the puddle awaiting him. Each stroke disclosed his desire to conquer any obstacles.

After our two-day erotic lock-in, he drove me to Dulles Airport. I wept like a baby strapped in a car seat, desperately trying to escape. He wiped my tears with the back of his hand.

We strolled slowly through the terminal, hands wrapped tightly together. We took small, concentrated steps, hoping that I would get a page from Mike, telling me that the problem was solved. We sat down at the gate, promises fleeing from our mouths like prisoners. We promised daily e-mails, phone calls, and fidelity.

Looking to Devin to comfort me, I discovered water in his eyes. Watching him search for every masculine hormone to entrap the emotion made me smile. We held each other until my row was called. He walked over to the boarding line with me. He kissed me. "I love you."

Wanting his words to be true, though my spirit was fiercely doubtful, I nodded. "I love you, too." I grievously headed through the tunnel. With every footstep, I could feel a piece of my heart crack. I mumbled to myself, "Life as a businesswoman is a bitch."

7

DEVIN

I prayed that God would keep my baby overseas until the raging bull was back in Arizona.

When I hit the campus, I went on the yard to drink with my boys. My body was missing the hell out of Clark, and I needed to drown out the feelings. The thoughts of withdrawal, weeks without my lady, depressed me. My alcoholic fraternity brothers were out on the yard, as usual.

One of my boys yelled, "Yo, where you been for the last few days?"

My boy Jason laughed. "He must've been with Clark's crazy ass, 'cause she didn't call me."

I said, "Whatever, man."

"Whatever, nigga. You know Clark be ringing my phone, harassing me when she can't find your punk ass." He looked at the other brothers. "Y'all know Clark don't play. Remember that time—"

Before he reminded us all, as well as shared it with anyone who may have missed it, I said, "Yeah, yeah. We all remember."

He was talking about the time when Clark showed her ass in front of entirely too many people.

When we'd finally finished pledging, we partied nonstop. We stayed on the yard, stepping and drinking. We would sit on the yard drunk, singing pledge songs until the wee hours of the morning. It went on for about a week before she went off. She supported my mission, but instead of concentrating on her when the process was done, I hung out with the dudes I'd seen every night for the whole semester.

I was so engrossed in my freedom, I inadvertently stood Clark up. I was on the yard, overintoxicated. The campus was unusually packed that night. Maybe it had something to do with us, the new guys, The Resurrection. We were like superstars, the tightest line to go over in five years. People surrounded us like we were giving away door prizes. High from all the excitement, submerged in my fame, I heard Clark's voice. I ignored my opportunity to chill. My arms were together over my head, covering my already tightly closed eyes. Grinding sexually, I chanted, "You ain't been licked, 'til you been licked by a—"

That's when I felt my collar choking me. Then I knew without a doubt that I heard Clark's voice. At this point, it was loud, real loud. Her little five-foot ass yanked me and cursed repeatedly. Realizing that it wasn't a dream, I put my arms down, stopped moving, and opened my eyes. Clark seemed to be the only person speaking, as if she had come in and put everyone on pause. My boys apparently saw her long before I did, because they were all sitting on the curb. We were the only two in the ring. I looked to my corner to seek coaching, and those punks just shrugged their shoulders as if to say, "You got some shit on your hands."

I followed her like a little puppy. She basically told the campus that I may be a dog, but I was her bitch. She certainly deserved to be treated better than that.

8

CLARK

I hate going to Europe. It's not the most hip thing to do for a single black woman. The white guys in the office die to come. I'm always forced. I'll trade my trips with anyone for little or no cost.

When I arrived, it was six-thirty in the morning. I caught a shuttle to the hotel. While riding, I looked at the gloomy, dirty surroundings. What's so great about Paris? It lacks glamour. My room was directly across the street from Restaurantes Flam's headquarters. The subway was just about two blocks away. Luckily, one train takes me to my favorite shopping strip, Champs Elysees. That's the only highlight of Paris for me. I end up spending all of my money on perfume and clothes. Surely, I wouldn't be seeing Champs Elysees on this trip.

Holding my cheek to the phone, attempting to feel closer, I desperately awaited Devin's greeting. Nothing. I couldn't imagine where he could be. It was almost one-thirty in the morning in the United States. I dialed the number over and over every fifteen minutes for an hour. Finally, I heard his loving tone floating through the line.

"Yo!"

"Baby . . ."

"What's up, baby?"

"I miss you."

"I know. I miss you, too."

I asked, "Where have you been?"

"Drinking with the bruhs. Trying to keep my mind off you."

It must be nice to be in an environment that helps relieve lovesickness. The laughter and music in the background made me resentful. He was carousing, while I awaited the moment to look into his eyes again. Suddenly, I got quiet.

I sighed and sarcastically said, "Must be nice."

Ignoring my obvious bitterness, he changed the subject. "So, how was your flight?"

"Long."

After he went on about his evening with the boys, I said my lonely good-byes and hung up. Although I was extremely exhausted, I got prepared for work. No time to be wasted. I was willing to work from sunup to sundown to solve the problem. Being there for my baby's graduation was the most important thing; sleep was secondary. It always takes me a few days to get adjusted anyway, so a few hours of rest wouldn't make much difference. I went down to a little café and got some coffee to help revive me.

I changed and headed across the treacherous road. People act like they don't see you. You have to really pay attention. They drive these little tiny dwarf-sized cars and zoom around like there are no driving laws.

After dodging traffic, I walked into the building. It appeared that the entire workforce knew I was coming to fix their problems. The key employees ran up to me saying all kinds of stuff. They talked too damn fast. I never had a clue what they were saying. They could have been calling me every bitch in the book. Regardless of what they were saying, I was looking at them like, "Never fear Super-girl is here."

After the petite little blond manager tried her best to explain the problem, she guided me into the test room. I tried to decipher the problem. They gave me a stack of test credit cards. The machine processed every card. For the first hour, I was unable to recreate the problem. Just about the time that I was ready to scream, "You Euro-jerks had me fly all the way here for nothing," I swiped a card, and the screen locked up. It wouldn't allow me to do anything. I wanted to cry. Unconsciously, I blurted out, "Shit."

After acknowledging that there was really a problem, I rolled up my sleeves. I loaded the original CD-ROM, hoping that some jerk over there had loaded the wrong version. If that was the case, I would have nothing to do except test the system. Wrong.

The original code contained the same problem. I began parsing through lines and lines of software code, trying to track down the anomaly. It could take months to find an error that happens sporadically. There was no specific sequence of steps that led to the problem.

I phoned the office and requested an urgent conference call. I explained the problem and asked that all the developers assist in finding the cause. After getting permission from Mike, I offered a cash award to anyone who found and solved the problem in the next two weeks. Sylvia, one of the sister-girl developers that I frequently chat with, blurted out, "Oh, I know why you are giving us two weeks."

She's cool, but has absolutely no class. I wanted to reach through the phone and smack the ignorance off of her face. Instead I didn't confirm or deny. I calmly stated, "Time is money. Now, I'll be working hard here and please do your best. Thanks."

Days went by with no word from the home office. There was less than a week left to find the error, implement a solution, and test it. It looked pretty bleak. To no avail, I worked twelve-hour days.

In my second week, it was obvious that I wouldn't be attending Devin's graduation. With a lump in my throat, I called.

"Baby . . ."

"What's up? You still haven't figured out the problem."

I sniffled. "No. I want to be with you on your graduation. This is just not fair."

"You know it's going to be all right. We'll go somewhere to celebrate when you get back. Wherever you want."

He tried to console me, but I felt like scum. "Baby, I'm so sorry."

"Clark, it's cool. Get some rest. Don't stress over the uncontrollable."

After coming to grips with not being home in time, I decided not to break my neck getting into work at the crack of dawn. When I strolled in late, there was a package for me, on my seemingly permanent desk. It was big, but rather light. It was from the home office, definitely a care package from Mike. He was famous for doing special things for his star employees. I opened the box and plowed through the tissue paper to find a CD-ROM with a note attached.

> *Clark,*
> *This CD works. I found the problem last week, but I've been testing it to make sure it works. Try it, test it, and give me what is mine!!*
>
> *Sylvia*

I loved her ghetto ass. My hands trembled like the CD was a vibrator. Never in my life had I been so excited about new software. I loaded the CD and stepped through the process nearly a million times. Everything worked. I showed the customer, and they were pleased. Only one request, they wanted me to stay until COB Friday.

Hell, no! Instead I swallowed the bitter thought and kindly responded, "Sure. Of course."

I called to see when I could get out on Friday and arrive in DC on Saturday. All I could get was a Saturday evening that would get me into DC at six A.M. on Sunday. Not the terms I wanted, but I could still make it to Hampton by 11 if I moved fast.

Problem-free for two days, I felt like an inmate being freed. When I got to the room, I packed and felt every second prior to stepping on the plane. My adrenaline pumped like an oil gage. No sleep desired. No meals necessary. Being able to attend Devin's graduation nourished me.

When I arrived at Dulles Airport, my nerves jumped around. The customs inspectors moved like turtles. My luggage seemed to be the last thing on the belt. Practically knocking people over, I grabbed my luggage. I waved down a taxi and was in my apartment by eight-fifteen A.M. I showered, got dressed, and hit the road by eight forty-five.

When I arrived, the procession had begun. From far away, I saw Devin stroll in. A fine-ass man, graduating with a four point oh. Who could ask for more?

When they started the recession, I pushed my way through the crowd, trying to get as close to the graduates as possible. As they exited, the ones I knew hugged me, and Devin's boys gave me handshakes. Devin seemed to be the last person in line. When Devin got into eye's view, he looked at me.

Definitely shocked to see me. Uncertain how to internalize his expression, I ignored my insecurity.

Running to him, smiling from ear to ear, I said, "Surprise, baby. I told you I was going to make it."

He half-heartedly hugged me, blatantly signaling that he wished I hadn't made it. Trying to decipher his reaction, I calmly asked, "What's wrong, baby?"

He forced a fake smile and said, "Nothing. I'm glad you made it. I wish you told me, though."

His comment made me feel a little more assured, but still something was strange. I continued to bury the questions lurking inside of me. Actually, I was interested in finally meeting my future in-laws. I demanded, "C'mon, baby. I wanna meet your parents."

"Okay." He didn't move. Instead, he looked like he wanted me to disappear.

Then I heard someone yelling, "Devin . . . Devin. Honey."

Devin nervously looked in the direction of the voice. Concerned about my baby, I looked at him. He looked like he had indigestion. He retrieved his hand from my grip. I turned to see who was causing this strained look to appear on my baby's face. A proud interracial couple approached us.

When he looked at me, I mouthed, "Are they your parents?"

With an attitude, he smirked. "Yeah, and . . ."

He spoke as if I'd said something negative. His mother was white, really white. Blond hair, blue eyes white. You could have bought me for a penny. Never, in a million years, could I fathom my Intellectual Thug being raised by a white lady. His obnoxious attitude baffled me. He looked like he wanted to run and hide.

Sure, I was vividly perplexed, but anxious to finally meet the people who reared such a loving man.

Devin hugged his mother and exchanged a few words. I grabbed his hand and tugged it a little, reminding him of my presence. Without looking in my direction, he began, "Mom, Dad"—nodding his head toward me—"this is my friend, Clark."

Friend . . . that shit stung like a hornet. I could have choked the life out of him. He demoted my status in front of the most important people in his life. The amount of emphasis he put on the word enraged me. It was as if he had shot a cannonball through my heart. Would a friend wash his dirty drawers? Would a friend cook, clean, and drive 130 miles every other weekend to see his ass? It took every drop of morality in me not to cuss him out in front of his parents.

By the unfamiliar expressions on his parents' faces, I knew they had never heard of me. His corny father turned to me, smiled gently, nodded, and shook my hand. His mother, with her long pointed nose and invisible red lips, twisted her face, cracking the pancake batter covering it, and reluctantly said, "Hi, nice to meet you, Claude."

She frowned and pulled her hand back, as if mine was contaminated. What a bitch. Wanting to make a good first impression, I smiled off my anguish.

She totally disregarded my presence, and so did Devin. I grudgingly released his hand. I stood there, feeling like a groupie with my own man. How? Why?

His mother grabbed his waist. "Honey, let's get going. We'll be late for our reservations."

"Okay." Then he impersonally turned to me. "Babe, I'll call you later. You going back home?"

"No, I'm here. Why would you think I'm going home?"

He proceeded to walk backward, impatiently facing me. Puzzled, I tiptoed toward him and grabbed the arm of his robe. His parents continued to walk, without even waving good-bye. I pleaded, "Devin, what is going on?"

"Babe, I'll hit you up later. We obviously need to talk. I'll come home when they get on the plane."

What was I supposed to say? I raised my voice, "Why are you acting like this?"

He put his index finger to his mouth, trying to calm me before his parents heard me. Why hadn't he told his parents about me? Why was I a big secret?

All the nights we lay together discussing our future flashed through my bewildered mind. How could he plan a life with me if I wasn't good enough to meet his parents? Did I not measure up? Did he think I'd embarrass him? Anger elevated the inflection in my voice. "Devin, don't act like I'm not standing here. Like I didn't practically swim across the ocean to get here."

I closed my eyes to trap the tears. Pulling the front of his gown, I tried to look into his eyes. "I have to mean more to you than this. You can't just walk away and tell me you'll hit me up later. What the fuck is up with you?"

"Baby, chill out. I'll be home tonight."

"Why tonight? Why can't I go with you now?"

He unemotionally spat out, "I'm not ready for you to be around them yet."

He shrugged his shoulders like I should understand. Instead, I flipped. "Fuck you, Devin. Don't come to my house tonight. Don't come to my house ever. Am I not good enough for you, huh?" I slowly accentuated my words. "How the fuck . . . can you say you love me and you're not ready for me to be around your family?"

He looked in the direction of his parents. "Like I said, we'll talk about it later, okay. Gotta go."

He bent down and kissed me on the cheek. I vigorously wiped the sympathy kiss from my face. He jogged off to catch up with his parents. I stood there, alone, watching my man and his parents disappear in the crowd. Wanting so desperately to run after him, tears of reality streamed down my face. I carelessly wiped my eyes, smearing brown makeup on the sleeve of my white suit. I slowly headed for the parking lot.

Embarrassed. Hurt. Shattered. I ran to my car. I sat there for a moment trying to internalize his words. I picked up my car phone and dialed Tanisha.

When she picked up, in between sniffles, I blurted out, "Devin's mother is white."

. Tanisha laughed. "Stop playin'."

"And he didn't even want to introduce me. His parents have never heard of me. He called me a friend and went to dinner without me. Like I'm some gutter bitch!"

"Girl, you trippin', right?"

Sniff. Sniff. "Does it sound like I'm trippin'?"

Feeling foolish, she said, "No, but . . ."

"But, Nish. It's obvious that he's ashamed of me."

"I don't think that's it." She tried to baby me. "Clark, I think he loves you. You ever think he's hiding them and not you?"

"No, why would he want to hide them?"

"Shit, why would he want to hide you?" She attempted to boost my ego. In her eyes, I am the most intelligent girl to walk the earth. She didn't realize that compared to the accomplishments in Devin's family, I am nothing. "You said his mama was white?"

"Yeah, but that ain't no reason to hide her. Shit, I don't care if she's a damn chimpanzee. She's his mother, and I want to meet her."

"Yeah, I don't know, Clark."

Anger etched away at my love for Devin as I sorrowfully drove home to be alone. How could I ever forgive him?

9

DEVIN

When I first met Clark, she told me that her dad was killed by a racist cop. How could I bring myself to tell her my mother was white?

Where I grew up, people either accept you as one or the other, not both. When I was in middle school, I dated white girls from time to time. Death threats taught me that it wasn't acceptable. I had to pick a side. Since I clearly look like a brother, I suppressed any trace of Caucasian decent.

At Hampton, thousands of miles away from home, I didn't tell anybody a damn thing about my heritage. I looked like everyone else. I strutted around campus like a proud black man, when inside I was a confused biracial boy. So many nights, I wanted to tell Clark, but I worried about her reaction.

Could I really handle Clark hating a part of me?

When I saw her run up to me at graduation, I could have released a cow from my ass. My disguise blew up in my face.

When I caught up to my parents, my mother asked, "Devin who was that girl?"

I mumbled, "I told you, a friend."

She looked into my distraught eyes. "I heard her cursing at you. What was that all about?"

How did she hear that? I looked at the ground. "Nothing."

She twisted her lips. "I hope you're not dating her. She seemed rather disrespectful."

My father jumped in to save me. "Leona, you just met the girl. How can you say that?"

"Frank, did you hear the words that came out of that young lady's mouth."

Dumbfounded, he responded, "No. I can't say I did."

By the time we got to the restaurant, I'd heard enough about Clark's dirty mouth. I felt weak for denying Clark. Finally the words I thought I'd never have to disclose came out, "Mom, that girl, Clark. She's my girlfriend. All the cursing you heard was because she wanted to spend the day with me."

"Devin, that's no reason to curse you out on your graduation. She doesn't sound like a really nice girlfriend."

My father nodded, agreeing with her.

"Would a nice boyfriend deny his girlfriend? Would he reject her on his graduation?"

"Well, Devin, if she was worth your time, you wouldn't have."

"I love her, though."

"You don't know what love is."

"I know I love her."

"So why is this the first we've heard of her."

She had a comment for everything I said. "Because . . ."

"Because of what, Devin?"

"I'on know."

I didn't have an answer. Who was I really ashamed of? My parents. Clark. Me. I wished I were stronger. Secure with my identity.

I stared at my menu. My mother cut the subject off with one last comment. "Devin, you're going on to professional school. You'll forget all about Clare."

I looked up at her and shook my head. She'd sized Clark up without even having a conversation with her.

10

CLARK

Everything in the apartment reminded me of the lie I was living. I took my clothes off, put them on the floor beside my bed, and climbed in. My sunny days were becoming cloudy with each passing moment. The cracks of my eyes released ceaseless tears, soaking the roots of my hair. I drifted off into a sobbing coma. When I finally woke up, my clock read 9:07 A.M.

I jumped out of the bed and ran for the shower. While the water from the steamy hot shower ran down my face, I wished I were sand being watered down until I was nonexistent. Visions of everything I wished weren't true haunted me. Devin hadn't called. He'd let me sleep on his rejection. He'd allowed it to settle within the depths of me. If he really ever loved me, how could he sleep knowing he owed me answers?

After a painful struggle, I put on the fake face and left for work.

When I got in the office, my coworkers wanted to know about my trip to France. I wished to God that I was still in France.

Mike came over to greet me. He escorted me to my new office and told me to relax and get settled. I didn't move one item from my cubicle. I sat there the entire morning, door closed, playing on the Internet. Every five minutes or so, it would hit me, and the salty water would start streaming again.

After lunch, I started moving. As I headed into the office with a huge box, I heard the phone ring. I stumbled around a chair, dropped the box, and darted toward the desk. I hastily picked up the phone. "Clark Anderson."

"Baby . . ."

My heart plopped into my empty stomach. I couldn't speak. A part of me wanted to run him off the side of the road.

"I'm sorry, baby. I know I got a lot of explaining to do. When can you come home?"

The bastard had enough balls to be in my apartment.

Finally, words escaped my locked lips. "I'll be there in a little while."

I moved everything from my desk into the office. My mind didn't allow me to organize anything. I rushed out of the office. By the time I got home, I was shaking like I had overdosed on caffeine.

When I turned the key, my heart thrashed rapidly at my breast. Surprisingly, I looked down to find it within the confines of my skin. Slowly, I opened the door, oblivious to my life's destiny, which hid inside. I walked in to find Devin sitting on the couch, staring at the blank television screen. His eyes were puffy like sleep was not on his agenda. I stood in front of him, weak, awaiting his explanation.

He started shaking his head. "Clark. I'm an asshole."

Arms folded, I relentlessly stared through him.

"I should have told you. I never expected us to get this far."

I twisted my head. "Get this far? When did you not expect us to get this far?"

"The first night we met."

Thoroughly pissed off, I put my hand on my imagination and shouted, "Bastard, that was two and a half years ago."

"I know, but we shared so much that night, that . . ."

"That what?"

He had the audacity to sound agitated. "Baby. Listen. Let me finish."

I sat on the far end of the couch. "When you told me about your father's murder, I was scared to tell you. Time just slipped away."

"Devin, what the hell are you talking about? What the fuck does my father's murder have to do with us?"

"Man, I mean . . . my mom's being white. I didn't think you could handle it."

A part of me felt relieved. Is that what this is all about? I laughed. "Devin, you mean to tell me that you were afraid to tell me your mother was white."

Sincerely, he shook his head. After spending an entire twenty-four hours checking myself, I couldn't stop laughing. "Devin, what did you think I'd say?"

He chuckled slightly, obviously realizing the whole thought was stupid. "I mean, I don't know how I would feel if one of my folks was a victim of racism."

"Devin, I was seven years old. I really don't remember, but I had to get over it. Hell, I can't go through life hating an entire race."

"Clark, I've seen a lot of shit in my life. I've seen people really trip over race. I didn't think you were like that, but I just didn't know."

I continued to giggle, but I still felt a sense of betrayal. I understood his issue with his mother's race, but his parents hadn't heard a damn thing about me.

"You know what. We don't even have to talk about that anymore. You know I am no racist, and I damn sure don't plan to leave you alone because your mother is white." I snickered at the thought.

I moved on to the real situation at hand. The reason I'd cried myself to sleep. "Devin, I understand why you chose not to tell me about your mother, but why don't they know anything about me?"

He looked at me like I was trudging on forbidden territory. I moved closer to him. He shook his head.

Sternly, I demanded an answer. "Devin." I raised my eyebrows as if to say, "Answer me!"

"You know, Clark, I don't know how to explain it."

I breathed heavily, turned my lips up. "Do the best you can."

He began, "Clark, for the last few years, I've been trying to tell you that my folks are hard to please. I didn't want to harp on it, 'cause I mean"—he stumbled on over his thoughts—"I was, um . . .

Man, I was just trippin'. I didn't want you to think it was a racial thing."

"Why the hell are you so hung up on race?"

"Man, being biracial ain't as easy as people think."

It was pitiful to see a grown man all screwed up about race, but he still hadn't adequately answered my question.

"Devin, you're right. I don't know about growing up biracial, but race has absolutely nothing to do with why you hid me. I'm confused." I raised my upper lip and rolled my eyes in my head. "You're not speaking coherently."

The whole racial hogwash started to sound like a bunch of rehearsed lines.

"Maybe I don't sound logical to you, but I know what I'm saying."

I looked at him in search of clarification. "Devin, make me understand. If you can't, how am I supposed to trust you?"

"Clark, for real, my mother is a bitch. I love her to death, but she's not an easy person to get along with. She would probably rip you to shreds if you sat down to talk to her."

"Devin, come on with that. You've told me in a million different ways that she's like that. Why did you think I couldn't handle it?"

He murmured under an impatient breath, "Clark, you don't get it. Do you?"

Why should I? I stretched my eyes widely and sarcastically answered, "No."

"It's easy for a black woman to deal with a black bitch. Tell me how a black woman deals with a white bitch."

He summed the argument up with that. I honestly had no idea. I'd never literally had to.

Certain of my not-guilty verdict after his closing argument, he got on his knees in front of me and wrapped his arms around my hips. He laid his head in between my legs and began to bite at my thighs. I pushed his head.

Why did he consistently swear his mother would tear me to pieces? What is wrong with me?

He looked up. "You forgive me?"

I mouthed, "Why should I?"

"'Cause I love you."

Before I could control it, I said, "But you're ashamed of me."

"Baby, for real, I'm probably more ashamed of me than any-body."

I leaned in and planted a kiss of forgiveness on his forehead.

II

CLARK

The summer came to a sudden halt. Devin put the last of his boxes into the car. How could I not work harder to find a job in New York? I dragged into the bedroom to grab my backpack. When I bent over, a sudden need to vomit came over me. I rushed into the bathroom. The cup of orange juice that I drank spilled out into the toilet. I continued to gag.

Devin ran in. He kneeled down beside me. "Baby, what's wrong?"

With an excuse for the tears in my eyes, I brushed off the situation. "Nothing, I think these new birth control pills are making me sick."

"Is this the first time you threw up?"

"Yeah, but I've been feeling nauseous all week."

He helped me up. I grabbed my toothbrush and proceeded to brush my teeth.

"You still up for going to New York?"

I nodded. Trying to convince me to stay home, he said "I'm just moving my things in and waiting for my furniture. I'll be back in a couple of days."

I rinsed my mouth out. No way was he getting rid of me so easily. "I know what you're doing, and I'm going with you."

"Aw'right. Let's go, then."

Devin had spent weeks searching for a place to suit his taste. After several dead ends, he found a cozy one-bedroom apartment about ten blocks from campus, right off of Broadway, on West 104th Street. The place is about seven blocks from Reggie. When we finally arrived in New York, I was mentally exhausted. Questions that I wouldn't dare ask trampled endlessly through my brain for the entire three-hour drive.

We double-parked outside of Devin's new residence. Devin and I proceeded to unload the car. After we removed all of the boxes from the car, we parked in the garage across the street. Devin suggested we grab a bite to eat.

We walked uptown. Restaurants everywhere. Devin put his hands on my shoulders and directed me to this little Italian restaurant. "Okay, I'm tired of walking. This is where we're eating."

I pouted. "I don't wanna eat here."

"Aw'right. Just watch me eat. I'm starving."

I laughed and pushed my elbow softly into his stomach. "Now, that's selfish."

"What's selfish is you walking up and down the street and not making a decision when you know your man is hungry."

"Whatever, Devin."

I proceeded to walk into the restaurant. A small-framed Italian man greeted us. "Just the two of you?"

I said, "Yes."

Devin interjected, "Actually, I'm the only one eating." He pointed to the menus. "So, we'll only need one of those."

I looked up at Devin. "Sir, he's being silly. We both need menus."

The host laughed. "Okay, no problem. Follow me."

We walked to a micro-mini table in the corner. When we sat, Devin's knees crashed into mine. I stretched my legs out and crossed them under Devin's chair.

"Thanks, baby."

I put my hands on his thigh and massaged it. "I know my man needs leg room."

"You're a trip."

"I'm serious."

We both looked at the menu. I couldn't decide on what to eat. I didn't want to eat. Still staring at the menu, I said, "Devin . . ."

He looked up.

"Are you going to miss me?"

He smiled. "Of course. What made you ask that?"

"I'm scared."

He grabbed my forearm. "Of what?"

"Of losing you."

He laughed. The waiter walked over. "Are you ready?"

Devin said, "Yes, I think. Baby, you ready?"

I nodded. He ordered. I ordered. The waiter took our menus. "Your meals should be here momentarily."

I smiled. "Thank you."

Silence.

"Devin, did you hear me?"

He sighed. "Yeah, but that's nonsense. We're not even going to entertain that today." He patted my thigh. "Okay We're going to be happy. I need you to be happy for me. Can you do that?"

"Yes."

"Good. No more silly talk today . . . this week. Okay?"

I rolled my eyes in my head. "Okay, Daddy?"

No laughter. No words. Somehow, a somber tone was set for our lunch date. After he devoured his food, he immediately asked for the check, paid, and we were out. Was it something I said?

"Baby, what's wrong?"

"Nothing."

"I just have a lot on my mind."

"Devin, before I said something about losing you, you were fine."

He massaged my neck with his thumb and index finger. "I'm fine now."

I wiggled away. "No, you're not. I've known you long enough to know when there is something wrong. You haven't said two words since you told me to be happy for you."

"Whatever, Clark. You hate when I'm quiet."

He put me in a headlock and began nibbling on my cheek. "Now, isn't that what the problem is? You want me to talk all the time. Huh?"

Welcoming his affection, I said, "Yeah, when you're quiet, I get scared. You know that."

"Clark, you know that's crazy." He released me from his grip. He pushed me. "I'm in love with a crazy girl."

I swung at him. "Stop! I'm not crazy. I just hate to think about losing you."

"Don't think about it, then. Your reality is only what you conceive in your mind." He grabbed my hand. "You're in control. Remember that."

"If you say so . . ." I sighed. How long could we really sustain this long distance thing?

After climbing three flights of steps to get to Devin's apartment, I wanted to pass out. I walked into the empty apartment and fell on the hardwood floor. My knees cracked.

Devin laughed. "My baby is getting old."

He climbed over me and stretched my arms behind my head. He pecked on my face. "You're a pretty old lady, though."

"Yeah and I'm your old lady."

He sat on top of me and took a deep breath. "I know." He shook his head. "I know."

I ignored his agitation. I pulled his head to me and kissed him. "I'm glad you know."

Devin rocked side to side. I screamed, "Ouch, be careful, this floor is hard."

He laughed. "I'm sorry."

I frowned and repositioned myself. "When does your bed come?"

He flipped me on top. He held my waist and lifted my body up and down. "Why? We can't make love unless we're in a bed?"

I giggled. "Oh, naw, I'll adjust."

We both laughed. "That's my baby."

I bent over and began kissing Devin's chest. He ran his fingers down my back, preoccupation in every stroke.

I aggressively summoned my man into the love scene. Physically he entered me. Emotionally he rejected me. I moaned loudly. My hips twirled vigorously. He lay silent. I closed my eyes to create a vision of reciprocity. My knees ached, pressed into the floor. Submerged in my pain and my fantasy, Devin stopped moving. I reluctantly opened my eyes. He smiled, "I'm done."

I slid onto the dusty floor and sat with my legs folded to my chest. I propped my chin on my knees. "Devin, what's up?"

"Huh?"

"What was that?"

He sat up and wrapped his arms around my waist. "Nothing's up, Clark. I've just got a lot on my mind."

He stood up. "Look at this place."

"But, Devin, that's what I'm here for. I'm here to help. I just feel like . . . as if I'm getting on your nerves."

He sighed. "I wonder why."

Damn. How was I supposed to respond? I didn't.

I slipped on my sweatpants and quietly began helping Devin unpack.

12

DEVIN

Radiant sunlight shining through the large bare window in my bedroom woke me. Getting through the night with a comforter on a floor was indisputably draining. I stood up to stretch out my long limbs. Clark moved. I tiptoed from the room.

Just as I opened the refrigerator door, I heard Clark's raspy moans. "Devin."

Damn. Why couldn't she sleep a little while longer, so I could have a few moments of peace? I ignored her and continued to pour my water. She called again. Finally, I answered, "Yeah, baby?"

"I ache all over."

I laughed. "Yeah, me, too. If the bed doesn't come today, we're going to a hotel."

She sashayed into the kitchen. Clark's beauty was still striking after a rough night's sleep. I smiled at the lovely sight before me. Morning breath barked, but I leaned down and kissed Clark's soft lips. "Hey, sexy."

She smiled. "Morning, honey."

I playfully ran my fingers through her hair. "I'm not used to living rough like this."

"Who are you telling? We're going to Reggie's place later, so we'll get a few moments of luxury."

I smirked. "I have too much to do. You can go without me."

"I already told him we were coming."

So what! Tell him that we changed our minds. Why do women always make plans without consulting their men first? Shit. The last place I want to be is sitting up with that obnoxious asshole. After a few swallows of water, I turned to Clark. "So, I guess you're going alone."

She pouted. "Oh, Devin."

I imitated her, "Oh, Clark."

She slouched her way into the bathroom. I could hear frustrated grunts over the running water. Her bratty nature was in rare form. I get sick of babying a grown-ass woman.

I walked into the bedroom and lay down on my pallet. My eyes studied the ceiling, as if my to-do list was written there. Clark entered the room quietly and kneeled beside me.

"Devin, you don't have to go if you don't want to."

I continued to look above. "I know."

"So, what are you going to do?"

I snickered. "I'm staying here."

She huffed softly and folded her arms tightly. I disregarded her funky attitude. I rolled over and closed my eyes tightly.

When I finally dozed off, a loud thump at the front door startled me. Before I could gain my composure, an overweight white guy was standing in the doorway of my bedroom.

"Is this the room we going in?"

With a trail of linen following me, I jumped up and headed for the living room. Dressed like she was going to work, Clark sat in Indian style watching the *Ricki Lake Show* like a statue. I fell down into her lap. I blew loud kisses. She pushed my head.

"Boy, leave me alone."

After several requests, she finally bent down and gave me an unaffectionate kiss.

The movers rapidly set up my new king-sized bed. I grabbed my sheets from the closet and started to fix my mattress. Clark followed me into the room. "Devin, I know you aren't going back to sleep."

Pretending that I couldn't hear her, I fluffed my sheets. She leaned on the frame of the door and hissed. After a moment, she shifted her weight onto one leg. "Devin, I thought you had a lot to do today. It's noon and you still haven't done anything."

I mumbled, "I'm about to get ready."

"Okay, Devin, whatever."

After I got dressed, I walked into the living room, and Clark was gone. Suddenly, my heart dropped. Where did she go? Why would she leave?

Her purse was gone. The television was on. In the middle of my investigation, she walked through the door with a small grocery bag. She looked me up and down. "Hey."

"Hey."

She walked in the kitchen and emptied the bag.

"What did you buy?"

"Ginger ale and crackers."

"You got what?" I walked into the kitchen to see if my ears were still working.

She rubbed her flat tummy. "For the nausea, remember?"

Hoping that was the explanation for her sudden crankiness, I asked, "How long have you been feeling like this again?"

Her weak eyes looked up at me. "For the last week or so."

I bent down and kissed her forehead. "Maybe you just don't want your baby to leave."

She buried her head in my chest. "Maybe."

She was as afraid of losing me as I was of losing her. I made one last attempt to secure our connection. I grabbed her hand. "Clark, just stay here with me. Quit your job. Follow your heart." I smiled. "Fuck it. Let's just live for today, for right now."

She tried to explain, "Devin, I can't. I don't want to be a burden to you. I can't."

"Clark, you could never be a burden to me."

She shook her head. "Devin, I'm scared. I'm scared to be here with you, and I'm scared to go home without you."

"So, what are you going to do?"

She danced around my question. "New York just seems so far away. But, it's no farther than Hampton. I just don't understand why I feel like this."

I shifted back to my plea. "Clark, we don't have to be in two different places. You know that, right?"

She nodded. I kissed her passionately. We fell to the floor and made love like it was our last time. Our bodies connected like pieces of a puzzle, a small portion of the big picture. She exploded all over me. Within seconds, she rolled over and quickly drifted off to sleep. I rushed into the shower and changed my clothes. I wiped my lady off and carried her into the bedroom. When I laid her on the bed, I grabbed my keys. She cleared her throat. "Devin, I love you."

"I love you, too. I'll be back in a few. I'm going to the bookstore."

13

CLARK

When Devin closed the front door, I hopped up and got the home pregnancy test from my purse. Five days late and I was losing my mind. The consecutive nausea in the morning didn't grant me any security. I prayed over the test before walking in the bathroom.

"Lord, please let this be negative."

After trickling on the little stick, I laid it on the sink and sat with my head in my hands. I slid my hands down and peeped at the indicator. Oh, shit! Two lines. I picked it up. This had to be wrong.

I grabbed the other test from the twin-pack. "Lord, I'm going to try again."

Again, I followed the same procedure. Damn. The same result. I paced the floor. Frantically, I called Tanisha.

"Nish, I fucked up."

"Why?"

"I'm pregnant."

She screamed, "You're what?"

I repeated, "Pregnant."

She tried to calm the hysteria. "Okay. It's not the end of the world."

"Yes, it is."

"No, it's not."

I tried to take deep breaths. "Yes, it is. Devin is going to die. His family is going to think I tried to trap him."

"Fuck his family. He made a mistake, too."

"No, he didn't. I'm on the pill. Not getting pregnant is my responsibility. I missed some days, like I always do, but this time I fucked up."

She sighed. "Clark, what do you think is best?"

"Nish, I can't have this baby. This is Devin's first year of law school. He doesn't need the stress."

"What does Clark need? How is Clark going to handle this? Devin is not the only one in this situation."

"I'll deal with it. I love him too much to add this to his life."

Why was I talking to Tanisha anyway? She doesn't believe in abortions.

"Clark, I'm going to say this, but you have to make your own decision. Everyone thought I should have gotten rid of Morgan, because Reggie was going to college and no one thought he could handle it. He handled it, plus he handled his business. Situations have their way of working out. If you decide not to have this baby, make sure it's what you want."

"Okay. Let me go. Devin will be back soon."

"Okay, honey. I love you. Call me."

I destroyed the evidence. How could I ever tell Devin? The thought of actually aborting a baby depressed me. How could I live with myself? Should I just move to New York? What if things didn't work out while Devin was doing the growth thing they say happens to men after college? What was a girl to do?

The door slammed. Oh, no! How could I look him in the eyes? He walked into the room.

"Hey, baby."

Was I really supposed to strip my man of the joy that was so clearly written on his face? Entrapping my confusion, I smiled. "Hey. What's up? Did you get everything you need?"

He plopped on the bed. "Yep. Plus I met a brother who's a third year. He put me down with all the first year professors. I'm pumped."

And I was pregnant. He showed every tooth in his mouth. How

could I remove the world that my man was propped so securely on? I smiled. "That's good. I'm so happy for you."

I bent down and kissed his lips. As if I needed to believe it myself, I repeated, "I'm so happy for you."

He hugged me. "Thank you, baby."

Devin gave in and decided to come to Reggie's with me. I rang Reggie's doorbell. Sheena flung the door open. "Hey, Clark."

She hugged me. "Hey, Sheena. This is Devin."

Devin reached out to shake her hand. "Glad to meet you, Sheena."

"Oh, the pleasure is mine."

"Where's Reggie?"

Devin and I walked in and sat on the sofa. Devin scoped the place. "Reggie's doing all right, huh?"

I smiled. "Yeah, he's okay."

Reggie bopped into the living room. Devin stood to shake his hand. "Hey, what's up, man?"

Reggie responded nonchalantly, "Nothing, man."

He turned to me. "Hey, Snook. What's up, baby girl?" He hugged me. "Sheena cooked dinner for y'all."

Did she really? I didn't smell anything. "What did she cook?"

She came from the kitchen. "I made lemon pepper chicken and rice."

How appetizing. Devin smiled at me. Her meal didn't appeal to our hearty stomachs. A Big Mac was more like it.

"Oh, good! I can't wait to eat."

"Okay, I'm setting the table now."

Reggie sat down on the chair across from us. We exchanged small talk. He refused to give Devin eye contact. He stood up. "C'mon, let's go eat."

We went into the dining room. Sheena and Reggie sat at the heads of the table. Devin and I sat across from each other. Sheena and I rambled about girl stuff. Devin stared into space. Reggie chimed into our conversation from time to time. Damn. Can't they talk about sports? What is it about Devin that makes Reggie so cold?

Sheena said, "Clark, I got a surprise for you."

She got up from the table and went into the bedroom. She returned humming, "We're going to the chapel and we're gonna get married. Going to the chapel and we're going to get married. Gee, I really love him and we're going to get married."

Just what I needed. I looked at Reggie to confirm. He smiled and nodded. Proud of his lady. Sure of his decision. I searched Devin's eyes for the same confidence. Pupils full with pressure, expanding in doubt, glared back at me.

Sheena stretched her arm out. "Look."

Reggie jumped in, "Two carat. Crystal clear."

I twisted my lips. "You are so cocky."

He joked. "Bling. Bling. You know how I do it."

We laughed. Devin peeped at the ring, but looked unimpressed.

"So, when is the date?"

They looked at each other. Sheena answered, "In about two years."

"What?" They're crazy. When Devin asks me, we'll be on a six-month plan. "Why two years?"

"I think you should live with someone for at least twelve months before you plan a wedding."

I spat out, "Why? That's ludicrous."

Devin chuckled, obviously agreeing with me. She sat down. "Girl, you have to live through four seasons with a person. You need to know how they react to change. Trust me."

And she always wants someone to trust her. She has all the answers, but something tells me that in this game, there are no rules.

I snickered, "Okay, if you say so."

Devin smiled. "Yeah, but she might have a point."

For the first time all evening Reggie responded to Devin. He slapped him a five. "Yeah, I think she might."

Sheena cleared the table. I looked at Devin. "Why do you think she has a point?"

Defensively, he responded, "I'm not saying that's the way we have to do it, but it makes sense."

Still not convinced, I sighed. "I guess."

How long should you take before deciding whether or not to bring a baby in the world? How about that? Who knew the answer to my dilemma? The seed of the man I love was growing inside of me, and I couldn't share the miracle with anyone.

14

CLARK

'Til death do us part. On the ride to Maryland, I chose to sleep, afraid to talk. What kind of daddy would he be? How would he feel if he knew? With each jolt of the brakes, I'd turn and peep at him, totally in control of our destiny.

We stopped in the Inner Harbor to eat at the Cheesecake Factory. The moment I walked in the door, nausea smothered me. The smell that used to entice me made me miserable. How could I tell Devin I needed to vomit again?

There was a sixty-minute wait. Oh, great. Devin and I sat outside on the brick steps. Fresh air calmed me.

When our buzzer rang, I dreaded walking through the strong aroma. The second I stepped through the door, I gagged. I tapped Devin's shoulder.

"Baby, I have to—"

I scurried into the rest room. Clear liquid spilled out on the floor just as I opened the door to the stall. A teenage girl looked at me as if I'd committed a crime. She frowned at her friend and said, "That shit is nasty."

They giggled and rapidly walked out. Did anyone ever think to ask me if I was okay? Shameful embarrassment forced me to tears. Why do I have to go through this alone? Speckles of vomit decorated my white sneakers. I sprinkled warm water on my face and rinsed my mouth. When I looked up, the reflection staring at me was pathetic. Frizzy loops strung from my ponytail, eyes red, and face pale.

Full of dread, I walked out to find Devin. He sat with a disturbed look on his face, tapping his knife on the table.

"Hey, did the waiter come yet?"

He shook his head no.

I proceeded to sit down. "So, what are you eating?"

He said, "The usual."

I asked, "What are you drinking?"

"Strawberry lemonade." He continued with the tapping.

"Devin, why are you tapping that knife like that?"

Abruptly, he stopped.

"Devin, what's wrong?"

"Nothing. I'm chillin'."

Why the one-word answers?

I asked, "Are you driving back tonight or in the morning?"

"What did I tell you?"

"I don't remember."

"Tonight."

I glanced out of the window. People walked in pairs, in laughter, in love. What about us? Wanting so badly for my man to spend just one more night with me, I sank into my seat and dropped my head.

"I have a ten o'clock class in the morning. I don't want to rush, so I'm leaving tonight."

"Okay."

He let out a pissed chuckle. "Clark, what more do you want from me?"

Stunned by his accusation, "What?"

"Clark, you've been quiet for three days. Every time I look at you, your eyes are watery. I'm trying to do my best. I just feel like it's never enough."

Refusing to disclose the truth behind my watery eyes, I apologized, "Devin, I know. I'm sorry. I'm just going to miss you."

"I'm going to miss you, too, but I can't handle the tears, the insecurity. It's going to drive me crazy. You have to be stronger." He paused. "You used to be stronger."

I placed my fingers in between his. "Devin, I'll be fine. I just need time to adjust. Okay?"

He wrestled my hand back. "Alright, man. Stop all that pouting."

I whined, "Okay."

Devin rushed me into the door, his boots grazing my heels. He wrapped his arm around my neck and moved my ponytail aside. Wet kisses burned my neck. He blew air to cool the fire. Shoved against the wall adjacent to the door, my arms and legs spread. Lock me up and throw away the key. He pressed his body into mine. I reached back and caressed his neck. He nibbled at my forearm. Flat against the wall, he reached down the small crack and rubbed my stomach. Then proceeded to grip my goodies in one hand. He pressed harder. I pushed my bottom into him.

"Oh, you wet as shit."

Flattered that he felt my love, I exhaled heavily. "I know."

Still glued together, we stumbled into the bedroom. He ripped my clothes off. I received him graciously. His passionate stare forced an immediate release.

He moaned, "Damn, baby."

Together, we glided. We drifted. We loved. Feelings so deep, sweat dripped profusely. Our eyes exchanged vows of love and commitment. Again and again, our bodies responded pleasurably.

After the eruption, we lay there overwhelmed with emotions. Devin broke the silence. "Baby."

I rose to my elbows. "Yes."

He rubbed my shoulders. "Keep loving me the way you do and you don't ever have to worry about losing me."

He pinched my cheek. "Okay?"

I smiled. "Okay."

He looked at the alarm clock. Suddenly, I felt sad.

"I have to get ready to get out of here."

No. Stay. Please, just one more night. Trying to appear cool, I said, "Yeah, I know. Are you going to be okay?"

"Yeah, I'll be fine."

He went in the bathroom to shower. I sat on the toilet and

talked to him, attempting to savor every second. Finally, he was prepared to hit the highway.

As we walked out to the car, we held hands. "Devin, I love you."

"I love you, too."

We embraced. He chuckled. "Clark, you're acting like we're not used to this. I'll see you next weekend."

I blushed. "You're right."

He kissed my cheek. "I'll call you from the highway. Okay?"

"Okay."

He got in the car. I slowly closed the door. The engine started. My stomach fluttered. In reverse, he pulled away. I waved. Slowly, he drove from the parking lot.

15

DEVIN

My head throbbed as I added ten additional chapters to my already twenty-chapter reading list. I massaged my temples as I scoped the room. So far, I could count on one hand how many black folk I'd seen in three classes.

With my workload, there was no way I could travel back and forth to Maryland every weekend. Immediately after class, I went to the library and buried my head in my books. After almost five chapters and twenty pages of notes, I checked my watch. Four hours gone. My stomach growled, but I was stuffed with schoolwork.

After my long evening of preliminary study, I felt like crying. Why didn't I take a year off? I sluggishly walked home.

Fully clothed, I stretched across the bed. Out for the night. The phone rang and startled me.

Clark sounded frantic. "Devin!"

"Yeah, baby?"

Her voice trembled. "Why haven't you been answering your phone? Why haven't you called me all day?"

Shit. My phone was on silent. I forgot to turn it on when I left the library.

"I'm sorry, baby. What time is it?"

She shouted, "Devin, it's one o'clock!"

My head was spinning as I attempted to sit up. "Why didn't you call the house? I've been here since nine-thirty."

"I did."

"Damn. I must have been out of it."

She sighed. "Yeah, I guess you were."

"Baby, I had a rough day. I'm sorry I didn't call. My fault."

Silence.

"Clark."

"Yes?"

"Baby, look, don't get upset. When I left class, I went straight to the library. When I got in here, I passed out."

Her impatient sighs made me feel my words were worthless.

"Clark, why the fuck do you have to flip every time I step out of line?"

A voice came through the phone. "If you would like to make a call, please hang up and try your call again."

Fully aware that she couldn't hear me, I yelled, "Clark."

I dialed her at home. The machine immediately picked up. How was I supposed to fall asleep with this childish drama on my chest?

16

CLARK

After pulling my hair out, worried about Devin, I had no choice. There was no way I could raise a baby in New York. Nor could I have a baby's daddy two hundred miles away.

I sat in my office with the door closed. Each time I began to dial the number to the Women's Clinic, I'd hang up. Finally, I found the courage.

"Arundel Women's Clinic."

I sat speechless. The receptionist repeated, "Arundel Women's Clinic."

"Uh."

"Hello."

"Yes, I'm calling to schedule a—" I huffed. "An abortion."

"Okay. What was the first date of your last period?"

Oh, great! Like I know that off hand. I speculated, "July fifteenth. I think."

She mumbled, "Okay, let me count." She continued, "That would make you about six weeks."

"Okay. So what now?"

"We usually like to schedule appointments around eight weeks."

Oh, no! Two more weeks of the tears, the regurgitation. "Do you have any openings two Mondays from now?"

She checked the schedule. "Yep, we have a nine-thirty. Will you be going to sleep?"

"Yes."

"Someone will need to accompany you to your appointment. Someone who can drive you home. Is that possible?"

"Yes."

"Don't eat or drink twelve hours before your appointment."

"Okay."

"And your name?"

Did she really need that? Reluctantly, I gave her my name. The appointment was scheduled.

As if I didn't have a million other things to do, I logged on to the Internet to see a six-week embryo. I stared at the screen and rubbed my stomach. I couldn't kill my baby. In the midst of indecision, my breakfast rapidly crept up. Uh oh! I pushed away from my desk and dashed into the rest room. As my insides fell out, I changed my mind.

When I got home, I climbed in my bed feeling lost, alone. I dialed Devin to apologize for my tantrum. His machine, again. Attempting to sound pleasant, I left a message. "Honey, sorry about last night. Call me when you get in."

The evening slipped away. Around ten o'clock, Devin called.

"Hey."

"Hey, Clark." He sounded pissed.

"Honey, I was feeling a little emotional yesterday. You know, PMS."

He huffed. "Oh, is that what it was?"

Trying to appear cheerful, "Yep. That's all it was. I was emotional, because I wanted to share your first day with you and . . ."

"You should have stayed here, then."

"Devin, I do have a job."

"You take off for everything else."

"I'm sorry, baby. I didn't even think about it."

"If you say so."

"So, Devin. How was your first day of class?"

"Long. Hard."

Searching for some interesting conversation. "Did you see the game last night?"

"I was studying."

"Devin. I'm sorry. I didn't mean to go off last night. I was worried. I was scared. And when I talked to you, it was like it never even crossed your mind to call me yesterday."

"I'm sorry you felt that way."

My attempts were not enough to invoke communication. Why did he even bother to call back? I tried on all the hats in my closet. Finally, I conceded, "Honey, when you feel like talking, call me back."

"Okay."

Wrong answer. He hung up the phone.

I called back. I begged, "Devin, please talk to me."

"Clark, I've been trying to talk to you, but everything I say is wrong. Every move I make, you question. Then, I tell you to stay, you say no. I don't know what you want."

"Devin, I want the best for you. That's what I want."

"The best thing for me right now is for you to be understanding."

"I can do that."

"You promise."

"I promise."

He talked freely for almost forty minutes. As if to drive a bulldozer over my mole hill of confidence, he said, "Oh, yeah, I'm not going to be able to come home this weekend. You're welcome to come up, if you want."

Restraining my anger, I said, "I'll let you know tomorrow. Have a good day."

I didn't humiliate myself and journey up Interstate 95. I decided to share my misery with Tanisha for the weekend.

It was late by the time I arrived in Baltimore. I didn't call, because I didn't want to wake Tanisha. She gets into the shop at six on Saturday mornings. When I got there, lights were out as usual. The kids were at my mother's. I stretched out on the couch and turned the television on. Within seconds, I realized I had entertainment. Thumping from Tanisha's bedroom. In between the loud thunder above my head, I heard Tanisha's voice screaming, "I love you so much." Sickened by the thought that my girl was down for the count, I irritably tossed and turned. Somehow, I managed to fall asleep in the midst of the madness. Awakened by footsteps on the stairs, I popped up. Then a voice so intimately familiar said, "Moe, I thought you cut the TV off down here."

Shit! There is only one person who calls Tanisha "Moe," short for her middle name, Monique. My brother. What the hell was he doing in Tanisha's bed? He and Sheena had looked like the damn Huxtables when I was there. How sorry? I felt betrayed for not being in on the secret love affair.

Waiting for some answers, I said, "She did turn it off." In an authoritative tone, "It's your sister."

Like a kid creeping down on Christmas Eve and hearing voices, he rapidly stumbled up the stairs as if I planned to punish him.

Suddenly, I heard the both of them coming down the steps. They walked into the living room prepared to confess. Tanisha was wearing a short green robe with her hair up in a ponytail, appearing well prepared for the visit. Reggie wore nothing except a pair of sweatpants and a look of humiliation.

Tanisha began first, "Clark, I hope you don't think I've been hiding something from you. This is the first time we have been together."

Trying to sound convincing, I lied, "I believe you."

Tanisha burst out laughing. "Trick, no you don't. You are trying to be cool for whatever reason."

Reggie added on to what I wasn't finding funny. "She always tries to act cool."

I wanted to remind him that he did have a fiancée. Tanisha needed to be reminded that she had a boyfriend, who carries a gun. Yet the two sexually satisfied fools thought everything was a joke.

I simply said, "Let me go back to sleep."

They walked into the kitchen, clearly confirming they didn't really want to hear what I had to say. Every second or so, I would hear a giggle escape the confines of the kitchen. I heard constant whispers, like they were hiding something from the kids.

In severe disgust, I slowly drifted off to sleep. When I woke up, the house was empty. I took a shower and headed straight for the shop. Tanisha's entire face glowed like a full moon.

She winked at me, which I found ironic. Just as I was about to blow up on her, I saw Fred walk out of the bathroom.

He came and patted my shoulder. "What's up Clark?"

"Nothing. What are you up to?"

"Trying to get everything straight with the building."

Tanisha gave Fred an agitated look. As if she was pleading, she said, "Freddie."

Demanding that he finish, I asked, "What building? Are y'all moving together or something?"

That would explain why Tanisha felt the need to get one last piece from the man that she really loves.

"Naw, I'm getting my baby a salon of her own."

Tanisha has been hiding too much from me. Have I been hibernating for so long that she just didn't get around to telling me? The look she gave him said, "Please don't tell." I felt more like an enemy than a best friend.

Dying to curse her out, I stared at her, but requesting forgiveness for whatever made her keep things from me.

She gave me an uneasy smile and said, "Give me a hug, Boo!" I slightly hugged her back. Then she pulled me closer and whispered, "I'm sorry."

Fred was so anxious to give me the 411 on the salon that he ignored the unusual exchange that occurred between us. He went on to describe the shop.

"Yo, that joint is going to be off the hook. It's 'gon be twice the size of this." He looked around the shop. "We 'gon have a day spa on the lower level. My moms 'gon open up her restaurant upstairs. It's 'gon be blazing."

He poked at me. "You try'n to work there?"

I shook my head. "I have a job. Thank you."

I was semiexcited about the salon, because it's what Tanisha always wanted. Reggie promised to help, but he wanted her to save some money. Show some initiative. Fred came along like a prince with a shining purse, carrying all of the capital to put Tanisha where she wanted to be. What was Tanisha giving up to receive the lavish gifts he brought forth? Why is she playing with fire?

After spending the entire day in the shop, forcing myself to bite my tongue, Tanisha came to her last customer, who was an older lady. We were the only ones left in the shop.

I blurted out, "Trick, what the hell is going on with you?"

She shrugged her shoulders and mumbled, "Girl, I don't know."

"What's up with you and Fred? Hell, what's up with you and Reggie?"

"Honestly, Clark, what happened with Reggie was not planned. I can go on with my life and pretend to be happy with a man who loves me, but the truth is Reggie is my soul mate."

Compassionately, I whispered, "Nish . . ."

"Clark, you will never understand. It's just that simple. You have never understood. I can't let him go. He can't let me go."

Wanting her words to be true and hoping that God could grant her her only request in twenty-five years, I tried to understand. "So, what did y'all talk about last night?"

"I asked him to leave Sheena, but he said that he couldn't. He claims that he loves her . . . and he loves me, too."

She sounded convinced. She actually repeated that ignorance.

"Nisha! I know you don't believe that shit. Do you?"

With the most angelic expression on her face, she said, "Yeah, I do."

"Well, why the hell did he ask Sheena to marry him?"

"I don't know. She's new and exciting right now. It will die off."

I shouted, "Tanisha! Snap out of it. They are getting married!"

"They are planning to get married."

"So, if you really think this is going to die, why are you wasting time with Fred?" I taunted, "Reggie's coming back? That's what you're saying, right?"

Tanisha shifted her weight onto one leg. She wiped her forehead with the back of her hand. Then she turned the lady around, completely disregarding my comment, and handed her the mirror. The lady barely glanced at the back of her hair, tossed the mirror back onto Tanisha's station, paid, and disappeared in a flash.

Tanisha started sweeping. I pressed, "Tanisha, what the hell are you doing with Fred if Reggie is coming back?"

When she looked up, her cheeks were soaked.

"Because my heart says he'll be back, but my mind says be smart. They say follow your heart, but my heart is leading me to a pair of empty arms in New York and off the Brooklyn Bridge."

She continued to spill her heart as she swept. "I can't explain it. Fred came in at the right time and told me the right things. He appears to be everything that I ever wanted, besides . . . well, you know. Initially, I was like fuck Reggie. As long as he is a father to his kids, I didn't care what happened between us." She paused. "Reggie never said he loved anyone else."

She held her stomach. "He has never been everything I wanted, but the little bit he gave me made me happy. I thought he was worth the wait. When he said that he loved Sheena, I tried to be tough and move on. And that's how I've gotten Fred mixed up in this."

She shook her head. "Last night, when I dropped the kids off, I didn't know Reggie was here. He didn't tell me he was coming. We started talking, and before I knew it, I felt like I needed him. I just wanted to hold him one last time.

"I've been lying to myself, believing that I was over him. Fred could never do to me what Reggie does. I care about Fred because he cares about me, but I love Reggie just because he's Reggie. He is the only man I will ever love."

I'd come to rectify the situation, but Tanisha had me bewildered. My only worthless advice was, "Just be careful."

17

DEVIN

I lay buried under a pile of books, disgusted with my decision to become an attorney. I considered bypassing the madness and becoming a receptionist at my parents' firm. In just two weeks, I was ready to quit.

My stomach growled to remind me that I hadn't eaten all day. I threw a pair of jeans on my funky behind and headed out. At the pizzeria on the corner, I waited for my order. People outside walked carelessly. No worries. They laughed. I thought about the multiple case studies due in the next few weeks. What I would give to be free. I grabbed my food and went home.

Once I gobbled down the last of my pizza, I called Clark. No answer. I imagined her legs up and someone dipping into my caramel. Furious with the thought, I called over and over again.

Trying to block the visions, I started working on my paper. Pictures of her naked body jumped out at me on my computer screen. I jumped up and paced around. How could I trust a woman who was so far away? No longer willing to face the thoughts plaguing my mind, I closed my books and fell asleep.

18

CLARK

I lay awake through the night, doubting my decision. How could I rob Devin of his rights? I got up sluggishly and ran to the bathroom for my morning ritual. I looked in the mirror. A murderer stared back at me. Doubt paralyzed me. The phone rang and startled me.

"Hello."

"Hey, baby."

"Hey, Devin. What's up?"

He sighed. "I missed you this weekend."

"I missed you, too."

"I just called to tell you that I'm definitely coming home Friday. I'm lonely without you. I think I'm getting a grip on this whole thing."

Was this the sign I needed to stop the procedure? Hang up, Clark.

"That's good, baby. I'm glad to hear that. I missed you, too, but I have to get out of here. I have a meeting at nine, and I'm not prepared. I'll call you later."

Apprehension in his voice, "Okay. Call me later."

I sat on my bed and rubbed my belly. We had plenty of time to have kids.

Tanisha knocked on the door. I dragged into the living room to answer. She wrapped her arms around me. "Clark, you ready, baby?"

In her arms, I felt safe. Free to let it go. I sniffled.

"Clark, baby. Are you sure you're ready?"

I sobbed. "I don't know."

She rubbed my back. "Why don't you wait? Take some time to think about it."

I rushed into my bedroom. With my purse in my hand, I headed out of the door. "If I don't do it today, it won't get done."

She pleaded, "You don't have to do it." She scurried behind as I skipped down the steps. "You need to think about what you want. Stop thinking about Devin. Think about Clark. If you do it just for Devin, you're going to regret it."

I ignored Tanisha's last petition. I pulled the handle on her car door. "Unlock the door."

Tears flooded her eyes. "Clark, please wait one more week."

"Open the door."

I sat in the passenger seat and refused to look at Tanisha.

We drove up to the clinic. Tanisha grabbed my hand. "You ready?"

I nodded. She sniffed. I took a deep breath and said, "Let's do this."

When I walked into the room full of young girls, I felt irritated like I was dressed in sandpaper. So many babies gone to waste. Does anyone really have a legitimate reason to abort?

I walked up to the receptionist. "Clark Anderson."

She smiled. "Okay, fill this out and have a seat. We'll need you to take a test when you're done. After that, hopefully we can get you back pretty soon."

"Okay, thank you."

The smug look on Tanisha's face as she stared around the room was that of disgust.

I chuckled. "Lighten up, Nish."

She gathered her composure. "Oh, I'm good."

After confirming that I was actually pregnant, they sent me into a room. Wearing only a gown, freezing, staring at white walls, there was no turning back. The doctor and nurse walked in. He explained the procedure. I lay back and closed my eyes.

I woke up in a recovery room. I didn't feel any different.

A short, chunky nurse tapped me. "Ms. Anderson."

Delirious, I answered, "Huh?"

"How do you feel?"

"The same."

She giggled. "And how is that?"

"Okay, I guess."

"Your sister will be back here soon. We'll wheel you to the car when she comes."

It was really over. My baby was gone. Reality finally settled in. Why did I do it? Trying not to upset everyone in recovery, I held back.

They helped me into Tanisha's car. I looked at this fool, and she was still crying. "Nish, you have to be supportive. I made a decision and it's done. We can't do anything now."

She sniffed. "I know. I'm sorry."

She took me home and stayed all evening. She left me asleep around eleven. Shortly after two in the morning, a baby cried inside of my apartment. I popped up, hustled into the living room. The sound got softer and softer. I tiptoed around. The medication had me chasing a baby that didn't exist, my baby.

I've heard my baby cry every night for a week. I sat in my apartment waiting for Devin, afraid that my nightmare would alarm him. Shortly after nine, the phone rang.

"Hello."

"Clark, don't be mad."

"What, Devin?"

"I'm not going to make it tonight, but I'll be there first thing tomorrow morning."

Content that I could have one more night to pray the dream away without company, I said, "Okay, see you tomorrow."

I pranced around, pacing back and forth anticipating Devin's arrival. I thought holding my man would force the sadness away.

Time slipped away. Four in the evening, no sign of Devin. I wanted to call, but I didn't. Did I really have reason for my insecurities? I'd sacrificed a life for his love, and he didn't have the decency to call and say he'd be late.

Devin's key finally jiggled in the door. I tried to appear calm. When the door opened, I didn't move. My eyes were directly on the television. When he stepped inside the apartment, he casually said, "Hey baby."

After a second or so, I huffed and turned to look at him.

He was scraggly. Hair grew wildly on his face. He walked over to the couch, sat down, and laid his head on my lap. He mumbled, "I miss lying on you."

He got comfortable. "Babe, I had a rough week." He rubbed his head. "Two case studies, an exam next week. I'm stressed like shit."

I listened intently as he bored me with the challenges of law school. He paused momentarily. After three entire weeks without visits, I looked down, and he was asleep.

I slid his head from my lap and went into my bedroom, hoping he would eventually come find me. I dozed off. When I finally woke up, it was eight o'clock. I walked out into the living room. Still he slept.

I yelled, "Devin!"

He didn't budge. After shaking him about ten times, he wiped his eyes. He sat up, still appearing half asleep.

My mind exploding with questions, I asked, "Devin, what's up?"

He squinted and gave me a disgusted mug. "What do you mean, 'what's up?'"

"I mean, what's up with you?"

He got up and walked toward the bathroom, letting his foul mumbles trail behind. I heard several "fuck this shit!"

I got up and stormed behind him. Before I could get to the bathroom door, it slammed. He slammed my door in my face. I banged on the door.

"Open the door, Devin. I'm just trying to have a decent conversation with you."

"Damn it. Can't you see that you're stressin' me?"

"Stressin' you? What the hell do you think you're doing to me?"

Stress. Living with murder. That's stress.

The bathroom door flung open, and he pointed his finger at me. "Clark, why the fuck"—he paused, so I felt the harshness in his words—"do you think I haven't been home in three weeks. I got enough stress. I don't need you talking that 'what's up' shit every damn time I talk to you.

"I'm trying to be the best damn man I can be, to a woman who lives damn near two hundred miles away." He nodded his head left to right, like an angry thug. "Shit, you chose to stay here, not me. Now, whatever obstacles we face, deal with it. Or just leave me the fuck alone."

I didn't cry. I just stood there. He stormed past me, grabbed his backpack from the floor in the hall, and went into the bedroom. I walked into the living room and began to contemplate the ultimatum that was presented to me. Sit back and be cool or let it go. Afraid to let go. Afraid to stay.

I walked in the room, prepared to reconcile. I looked down to find Devin on his knees praying. I walked over and kneeled beside him. After all, a family that prays together stays together. I held his hand as he continued to pray silently. I said a prayer for forgiveness, for betraying Devin and disregarding the life of my baby.

When he finished praying, he rose to his feet. We looked into each other's eyes and didn't say a word. The anger and distress we both had boiling inside evaporated. I hugged him, and he casually returned the embrace.

I began to talk. "Devin, about the ultimatum . . ."

He covered my mouth with his entire hand. "Let's not argue. We're both stressed right now. Let's go out to eat."

19

DEVIN

When I got back to school, there were approximately ten messages from my study partners. When no one picked up, I ran to the library. As I was leaving, I ran into Jennifer. She was the quiet, lonely type. Almost certain that she didn't know the answer, I pressed my luck. "Have you seen the other guys in our class? We were supposed to be studying together."

She smiled as if to say, "You know I don't deal with you people like that." Then she spoke softly. "No, I haven't seen them. Do you need a study partner?"

Totally oblivious to her come-on, I took it as an insult. "No, I don't need a study partner. I just find information exchange a little helpful."

Totally ignoring my sarcasm, she said, "Oh, I was just going to say that we could study together."

Elated that she'd disregarded my comment, I agreed. My argumentative mood could probably be attributed to being with Clark for twenty-four hours.

We decided to go to Jennifer's place, because she stayed about a block away from campus. For the first time since school began, I really looked at her. She was a little thick, more of an athletic build, yet there was something sexy about her. She wore a black leather jacket, a pair of skin-tight jeans, and black leather boots. She wrapped her face and neck with an elegant black velvet scarf.

Her long, curly sandy brown hair blew wildly as we trudged toward the wind. Her cheeks turned red, and her suave walk turned me on.

My nature began to mess with me. The entire two blocks, I was thinking, "I can get it."

I made a promise to myself that I would do absolutely nothing except study when we got to her place. She opened the door to a huge empty apartment. There were big throw pillows spread around the room with candles in various places. Pictures were displayed on her refrigerator, held by magnets. There was a family photo, which shocked me. She was on the photo with a white couple and two younger white kids. Unlike me, Jennifer was clearly biracial. I hoped that one day she would explain the inconsistencies in the picture.

She immediately gave a disclaimer. "I'm getting furniture soon, but have a seat on the floor for now. Okay?"

She noticed me looking at her pictures. I attempted to hide my confusion, but she walked into the minikitchen and casually said, "I'm adopted."

She made her statement like she'd become accustomed to the ignorance. It's typically the same reaction I get when people realize my mother is white.

There was something so innocent, yet mysterious, about Jennifer. She offered only small portions of herself. It killed me that she hadn't given up any information in an entire walk. Finally, after fumbling around the apartment for almost ten minutes, Jennifer joined me on the floor, holding a cup of hot tea in her hand. She opened her notes, and we began an intense study session.

After hours of schoolwork, I decided to put in some personal time. I stood and began to stretch. "So, who's the lucky man?"

"What?" She laughed shyly.

I broke it down in layman's terms. "Where's your man?"

Softly, she replied, "I don't have a man."

I consoled her with the most common reply to her statement. "I can't believe that."

"Believe it. Just me, myself, and I."

I asked, "When was your last serious relationship and why did y'all break up?"

So peacefully, she said, "He cheated." She paused. "Repeatedly."

Going in for the steal, I said, "On you? That's unbelievable."

She smirked. "Why? All men cheat, given the right time and opportunity."

Maybe she had a point but I proceeded to defend men. "Not all men cheat."

"Do you have a girlfriend?"

Never had I had the desire to lie about Clark, but I considered it. "Um, yeah."

"Have you ever cheated?"

"Nope."

She looked sad, as if she hoped I did. "Wow, that's pretty good, Devin."

We chatted about relationships for another hour. I decided to get out of her place before my time and opportunity arrived sooner than I expected.

As I headed toward the door, Jennifer asked, "So, are we study partners now?"

"Most definitely." I smiled and walked out.

I caught a taxi to my place. When I gave the driver my destination, I dialed Clark on my cell phone.

She picked up. "Hey, baby . . ."

"Hey, I meant to call you, but . . ."

"That's cool. I'm just getting in myself. Tanisha and I went to Jaspers for dinner."

Momentarily dreaming that my Clark had returned, I didn't mumble a sound.

"Baby, are you okay?"

Not wanting to ruin the rare, peaceful moment that we were sharing, I decided to end the conversation.

"Yeah, baby, I'm just really tired. I'm gonna go in here and pass out."

"Me, too."

"I love you, and if you can't sleep, call me."

"Okay, I love you, too." She hung up the phone.

My prayers were answered. All the sexual fantasies that I was having about Jennifer were useless. I held my phone tightly, hoping that the person on the other end would stay that way forever.

20

CLARK

The sun beamed through my sunroof as I impatiently sat outside of Tanisha's new salon. She called me from the settlement to say she and Fred were on their way. From my analysis of the exterior, it needed a lot of work. Tanisha had asked me to do the interior design, and I gladly welcomed her offer. Extra curricular activities were the outlets.

My skin felt moist and clammy. Tired of waiting. I closed my windows, started my car, and turned on the AC. As I attempted to recline my chair, Fred beeped his horn. Immediately, I jumped up and got out of the car. Tanisha had a look of disbelief as if she'd awakened in the midst of a wet dream. My heart danced joyfully as she jumped from Fred's jeep, holding the key up in the air.

"Congratulations, girl!"

She ran to me, wrapped her arms around me, and spun me in an infinite circle. She sang, "Clark, can you believe it?"

"Yes, I believe it. I'm so happy for you."

She covered her mouth with her right hand and extended her left. "Look . . ."

She exposed a beautiful emerald-cut diamond set in a white-gold band. What the hell? Dating was one thing, but marriage? He was illegal.

Fred walked up behind me before I could actually internalize it. He put his hand on my shoulder and said, "You like it?"

Trying hard to conceal my disgust, though it wasn't working, I asked, "When did this happen?"

Tanisha blushed and batted her eyes. "After settlement."

Attempting to sound excited, I said, "Give me the details!"

She painted on a fake smile and began the details of their fraudulent engagement. "Girl, right after I called you, my Realtor jogged behind me. She yelled, 'Ms. Simmons, you forgot to sign this.' I grabbed the document and . . ."

She handed it to me. I looked at the sloppy handwriting on a piece of stationery. It read:

> *I, Fred J. Wilkins, have never loved anyone the way that I love you. I knew from the very second I saw your face that you were the woman for me. Today, as we start this partnership, let's agree to be partners forever. You have changed me in ways that you don't even know. I want you to be my wife, the mother of my kids. I love you. Will you marry me?*

I raised my eyebrows. "And you said?"

She rolled her eyes at me. "Trick, I said yes."

I faked a cry to appease my girl. "Aw . . ."

We walked into the new building. Tanisha and Fred held hands like partners. A part of me envied them, walking into their new building that they had purchased together. After we finished talking about what we planned to do with the shop, Tanisha got in the car with me because Fred had something to do, which was the story of his life.

When Tanisha closed the door, I could not wait to get the unedited version. She began, "Clark, damn it!"

Shocked by the words exiting her mouth, I asked, "Why are you saying damn it?"

Her teeth clenched together. "Because, damn it! I wasn't expecting Fred to ask me to marry him. I'm not ready to get married."

"Why the hell did you say yes?"

"Shit, have you ever had someone ask you to marry him? It is the most flattering thing you can imagine." The glow in her eyes dimmed. "How could I say no?"

Momentarily, I fantasized about Devin asking me. I couldn't dream of saying no, but I loved him. "Nish, if you don't love him, it won't work. No matter how flattering his proposal is. That is only the beginning. You are making a commitment to be with this man for the rest of your life."

She smirked. "Well, shit. What should I do, say no?"

"Do you love him?"

She rolled her eyes in her head. "Yeah. Kinda."

"What kind of answer is that?" It upset me that she was taking it so lightly.

"Well, he treats me good, and I don't think I ever wanna *really* love anyone again. When Fred goes out, I don't worry. I don't feel insecure. I don't know if that's because I don't love him or if it's because he does everything to make me trust him. Whatever it is, I like the feeling. I spent so many years hoping Reggie would eventually give me his all. I waited patiently, and in the end, my love didn't pay off. So does love really matter?"

"I think it does."

"Girl, listen, I'm never gonna love another man like I love your brother, so I may as well marry the man who loves me."

After experiencing real love for a man, I couldn't imagine how anyone could be happy any other way. She looked like the football captain had just asked her to the prom, but not like a woman about to marry the man she loved. She and Fred had parted just hours after he popped the question.

Refusing to accept it, I asked, "So, are you going to go through with it?"

"Yep."

"What about his other affiliations?"

She smirked.

"I mean, you do have kids involved, and if he . . ."

"Clark, Fred has been putting things in order since he met me, so that he can make a clean break."

"And you expect me to believe . . . I mean, you believe that he's really going to get out of the game."

"Clark, Fred is focused. He makes enough money managing the other salons to make me happy. With my salon having a spa and a restaurant, he doesn't have to hustle anymore." She tried to persuade me. "He is getting out of the game."

"Well, all I'm saying is that my niece and nephew are a part of this transaction, too." I grabbed her hand to assure her that I was sincerely concerned and not just trying another spiteful tactic to keep her from happiness. "So, please make sure he is really free of all associations before you start planning a wedding."

"You know I'm not stupid. I am definitely not going to marry a hustler."

Jokingly, I said, "And if you get stupid and decide to marry a hustler, I'm gonna kick your ass and take your kids."

21

DEVIN

With such a humbling beginning, I never thought I'd find myself at the end of my first year. I invited the rock to my law
school salvation out for a drink. We went to an Irish pub on Fifth
Avenue on the Upper East Side.

With my shot of Hennessy raised, I said, "Here's to one year
down and two to go."

Jennifer tapped my glass with her bottle. "Here's to the summer."

We gulped our drinks. "Now, that's the truth."

"Devin, at least you can look forward to sharing your summer
with someone. Poor me, I'll be here all summer alone."

"Not really."

"Why do you say that?"

I took a deep breath, disgusted with myself. My parents had offered me an internship that I could not refuse for the summer. I
turned down my internship in D.C., but Clark hadn't the slightest
idea. As I rambled to Jennifer, I hoped that she would help me
find a solution that both Clark and I could live with. I ordered another shot of Hennessy and disposed of it quickly. Jennifer shook
her head. "Devin, drinking isn't going to solve it. Just tell her. The
longer you wait, the worse she'll react."

"You don't know Clark. Do you?"

"No, but I do know women."

"What would you say if your man told you he was only staying with you for three weeks, when you thought he was coming home for the summer?"

"It depends on the circumstances. If it would benefit his career, I would support him."

I smiled. Maybe Clark would feel the same.

Clark picked up the phone. "Hey, honey."

"Hey." I cleared my throat. "What's up?"

"I'm waiting for my man to come home."

Damn. Could she have at least given me a few seconds before diving into that topic?

I sighed. "Clark."

"Yeah, baby. What's up?"

"Say you won't be mad."

"Devin, how the hell can you say that? If you say something to piss me off, you know I'll be mad."

I jumped on the wrong side of the fence and the bulldog was off his leash. Letting not another second pass, I confessed. "Clark, my parents offered me a position that no other law firm would give a first-year law student. I'll actually be—"

"In Arizona."

"Yeah, but it's a great opportunity. I . . ."

She chuckled. "Devin, who do you think you're fooling with that great opportunity bullshit? You're going to work for your parents when you graduate, anyway. And I'm certain you'll have the same position if you never do an internship."

Did she ever think that I wanted to have experience when I start practicing?

I mumbled, "Whatever."

She angrily replied, "Whatever?"

"Yeah, Clark, whatever. Whatever you say, but I'll be in Arizona for the summer. You're welcome to come out for a few weeks, if you want, but that's where I'll be." My balls felt huge.

She calmly asked, "So, when are you leaving?"

"In three weeks."

"Are you staying with me until you leave?"

"Of course."

22

CLARK

I doodled in my notepad during the weekly staff meeting. My team leads gave their status, while I daydreamed about my relationship. Was I waiting in vain? What were the chances that Devin is really faithful? Seeing him twice a month is not enough. Long-distance relationships are for fools. I was tired of hanging in smoke-filled clubs, talking to jerks, when all I really wanted was to have a man at home on a consistent basis. I wanted and needed more.

After waiting patiently for nine months, he slaps me with his decision to go to Arizona.

Steve, the database team leader, pounded on the table. "Earth to Clark. Earth to Clark."

The team laughed as they gathered their things. "Okay, is everyone done?"

Some nodded. Some said, "Yes."

Happy to finally be alone, I rushed into my office and closed the door. Just when I thought I had a grip, something else arose. Could one woman really have it all? A career. A man. Happiness. My relationship with my man always conflicted with my job. How could men control so much of our sanity? I paced around my office, rehearsing what I planned to say to Devin.

"Devin, I think I want to see other people."

Too harsh. I tried multiple attempts to make it sound better, but there was no nice way to let it go. By the time Devin finished law school, I'd be twenty-seven. Anything worth having would be taken. I decided to take advantage of my options while the ocean was still full. Why was I so lonely when I was supposed to be in a relationship?

Devin called from his cell phone to ask me to help with his things. Reluctantly, I walked out to greet him. Devin stepped out of the car. "Hey, baby."

With my lips twisted, "Hey."

He grabbed me. "Damn, can I get a hug?"

I barely hugged him. He pulled two trash bags from the car. "Here."

"What's this?"

"Dirty clothes. I haven't washed in weeks."

With total disregard for the clothes inside, I dragged the bags across the parking lot and up the stairs. He yelled out, "Be careful. They might burst."

My intentions exactly, seeing him run around doing a scavenger hunt for his socks and underwear. Unfortunately, the hefty bags were well intact when I pulled them into the apartment.

Devin walked in behind me, carrying his oversized duffle bag and rolling a medium-sized suitcase.

"Is that everything?"

He nodded and walked into the bedroom. His boots, loosely tied, dragged. Damn, that shit turns me on. I followed. He dropped his bags and sat on the bed. He opened his arms. I stood in between his legs and hugged him.

He pouted. "You mad at me."

Trying to avoid confrontation, I lied, "No."

He kissed my cheek. "Yes, you are. I can tell by the way you looked at me when you came outside."

"I'm not mad, just a little disappointed. Maybe, I'm just confused."

I kissed him, but felt resistance in his response. I pulled back. "What's wrong?"

He shook his head. I tried again. He pulled away. "Clark, I don't know."

After I'd already convinced myself that I wanted out, the rejection I felt made me long for him. I begged, "Devin, what don't you know?"

"I don't know about us."

"Why?"

Suddenly, it felt like my whole world would crumble without Devin.

"Because it's too hard. I'm not giving you what you deserve."

Afraid of accepting the truth, I lied, "Yes, you are."

Now, on my knees in front of him, I pleaded, "Devin, you're all I have. I can't let you go."

He rubbed my hair. "It hurts me to hear the disappointment in your voice when I can't make it on the weekends. I know it hurts you, but I'm only one person."

"Devin, I know. I've been cool all year. What are you talking about?"

He held my hands. "Clark, I know you're not happy."

He searched for excuses to leave me, but damn if I planned to let him go so easily. "Devin, I am happy. I love you."

He rubbed my eyebrows. "Are you really?"

I nodded. "Plus, you said the first year is the hardest. We made it through that." As to convince myself, "We can't give up now."

"You got a point, baby." He pounded my fist with his. Official.

Three weeks passed like minutes. Devin rushed to pack. I watched him. Questions about our future lingered in my heart. As I suppressed the urge to cry, the initial anger I felt when Devin told me his summer plans returned.

With his duffle bag on his shoulders, he stood in front of me. "I wish you could come with me."

I giggled to myself. He needs a bimbo with nothing else to do except follow him. I have a career that he totally disregards. To flatter him, I said, "I know. I wish I could, too. But, I'll come out for a weekend or two."

He kissed me. "I'll call you when I get to Phoenix."

"Okay, baby."

He closed the door, and I opened my heart to search for love elsewhere.

23

CLARK

A few days after Devin left for Arizona, Tanisha threw a birthday party for Fred at a private club in Baltimore. I pulled my hair into a ponytail. I wore jeans and a fitted T-shirt. Though I was open to meet new guys, I knew my type would not be in Fred's circle.

I went to the party rather early, planning to help Tanisha get things together. Then I could sneak out when it began to get packed.

When I got there, the parking lot was packed. What kind of party starts on time? I walked in, and a bunch of guys, obviously on the other side of the law, turned to greet me.

I mumbled, "Hey. Where's Tanisha?"

They replied randomly, "Back there."

After I passed, they began to *ooh* and *ah*. I heard a few, "Shorty phat as a motherfucker."

Disgusted by their lack of respect, I concluded it would be a short night. When I finally bumped into Tanisha, I asked, "Who are those assholes up front?"

Totally dancing around the fact that I felt they were jerks, she smiled. "They're Fred's buddies."

I turned my face up. "Oh . . ."

She laughed. "Loosen up. They're cool."

I didn't respond. We set up the food and put up a few decorations. Slowly, more people began to straggle in. The DJ began playing that head-throbbing House music. Finally, after an hour or so, Fred walked in with his entourage. It appeared we were the only females in the club.

The guys with Fred were all nice-looking guys. The finest brothers are the ones who don't work forty hours a week.

Fred walked back to us. He grabbed Tanisha and held her tightly. He gazed into her eyes. "I love you, baby."

A few of his buddies stood close by. One in particular caught my eye. He had a beautiful, even, dark brown complexion. His shape-up looked as if it had been done with a straight razor. He laughed and chatted with his friend. His radiant smile sparkled across the room.

Fred grabbed my arm and began to dance with me. "Clark, I'm glad you're here, baby."

"I wouldn't miss it for the world," I lied.

We danced as a little trio for a moment. His buddies started filling the dance floor. Suddenly, the club appeared packed. Some of the stylists from Fred's salons began to show. They flirted with the would-be ballers. I danced alone. Money was being thrown around at the bar like dice.

When someone would look at me, I'd immediately turn my head. They would move on to the next available candidate. Tanisha floated around, chatting with everyone, thanking people for coming. I stood off in a corner, sipping on Hennessy.

Someone slipped up behind me. He bent down and whispered in my ear. "You must be Clark."

Agitated by his approach, I turned around and took a step backward. It was the guy who I'd noticed earlier. Instead of brushing him off, I smiled. "Yeah, and you would be?"

He blushed. "Troy."

Afraid of the attraction I felt, I repeated, "Troy."

He laughed. "Yeah, Fred speaks very highly of you."

I was shocked. "Really?"

"Him and Tanisha."

I never heard of Troy. Why would they discuss me with him? I noticed a diamond-studded platinum bracelet on his wrist. It was obvious that no matter how fine he was, I should back up.

"Where do you know Fred from?"

"It's a long story. Fred and I go way back."

Bad sign. "Is that right?"

"Yeah. I've known Fred for about ten years."

I tightened my lips. "Really."

"Yeah, went to barber school together."

"Fred went to barber school?"

He nodded. "Yep."

"I didn't know that. So do you cut hair or did you decide to stop as well."

He chuckled. "Yes. I still cut hair."

He pulled out a business card and handed it to me. "I own a few shops, but this is where I actually work."

Approving of his profession, I smiled. "Okay, so I know where to come to get my hair cut."

He rubbed the top of my hair. "I wouldn't dare cut all this pretty hair off."

"Whatever."

We laughed, and he grabbed my empty hand. "You want to dance?"

I began to move to the horrible beats blasting out of the speakers. He bent down. "Clark, I'm not even going to front. I want to take you out."

I nodded. He continued, "Honestly. I've been asking Tanisha when I could meet you since I met her."

"Why me? What do you know about me?"

"You know guys always ask their boys' girls if they have any friends, right?"

I shrugged my shoulders. "I guess."

"So I asked Tanisha. She told me none of her friends were available. Then Fred told me about you."

Confused as to why Fred thought I was free, I asked, "And what did he say about me?"

"He said you were in a relationship, but your man lives in New York."

"Yeah and . . ."

"And he said you were fine as shit. And you're definitely that. So, why is your man in New York?"

Jumping to my man's defense, I said, "He's in school."

"I know, but you can't leave a fine young lady like you home to wander."

"I don't wander. I'm faithful."

He did a swift turn and danced as if he was teasing. "Is he?"

I didn't answer. I didn't know.

He proceeded, "That's what I mean. That's where a nice guy like me comes in the picture."

Stunned by his confidence, I asked, "So you think you're in the picture."

"I would like to be."

We danced in silence for a moment. Why shouldn't I go on a date?

"So, can I just take you out to dinner?"

"We'll see."

"I'm a patient guy. Just let me know." He reached out for a hug. His body felt warm and inviting. I could feel his muscles through his shirt.

Unconsciously, I groaned. He smelled so good. I could eat him. Seemingly aware of my thoughts, he smiled, caressed my shoulders, and said, "Before I go, do you want something from the bar?"

No, don't go. Stay here. Hold me. Flatter me. Flirt with me. "Why are you leaving so soon? You just got here."

"I just stopped by to show my man some love, but I'm tired."

Left speechless, I nodded. "I definitely understand that."

"So do you need a refill?"

Prolonging his departure, I rapidly guzzled down the Hennessy in my glass and said, "Yep."

On our way to the bar, he stopped and asked Tanisha if she wanted another drink. We stood at the bar. My shoulder touched his upper arm. I looked forward. His eyes concentrated on me. He twirled his finger in my ponytail. "Clark, you are so cute."

"Thanks."

He ordered our drinks. "I'm not trying to steal you from your man. I just don't want a pretty girl like you home alone."

Uncertain of my relationship status, I kidded, "Are you sure about that?"

"Clark, I don't steal nothing that doesn't want to get stolen."

He handed both Tanisha's and my drinks to me. He tipped the bartender twenty dollars for a shot of Hennessy and a draft beer. He bent down, kissed me on my forehead. "Clark, you got my number. I hope you use it. I'm out."

And like that, Troy was gone. I straggled over to Tanisha, upset with myself for being flattered by one of Fred's low-life friends. I handed her the beer.

She had a sly grin. "You like Troy, don't you?"

"Girl, please."

One of the stylists who works with Tanisha chimed in, "Girl, Troy is fine as shit."

I gave her a high five. "You ain't lying, but he's not my type."

She added, "Girl, everybody likes Troy. He is a sweetheart. Everyone he messes with falls in love with his fine ass. I hear he knows how to treat 'em. Plus, I heard he ain't no joke in the bed either."

As if she knew I was curious, Tanisha shouted, "And he's legal."

I blushed. "Really?"

Had I known that, I would have given Troy more play. I was impressed with his approach. He'd confidently stated his intention and rolled out.

Tanisha said, "Yeah. He has been trying to get me to set him up with you forever, but I keep telling him that you're in love."

"Why haven't you ever said anything to me about him?"

"I don't know. He's fine and all, but you're so wrapped up into Devin, I didn't think you'd be interested."

"Well, I just might be. Devin ain't the only man on earth. And besides, I get lonely, too."

She slapped me five. "Now, that's the Clark I used to know."

24

CLARK

My trip to Phoenix arrived a lot sooner than expected. I re-
sisted the urge to call Troy. Afraid that he could talk my
panties off and Devin would know.

When the plane landed, I felt sick. I feared that a butterfly
would fly from my mouth if I parted my lips. Devin was nowhere
in sight, which only helped to increase my nerve activity. Finally, I
heard my baby's voice, along with the sound of feet rapidly pat-
ting the floor. "Clark."

I turned to find my baby holding two dozen red roses. He
hugged me and practically swallowed my tongue. I felt loved.

When we walked out of the airport, the heat virtually smothered me. Everything was blurry. Steam rose from the ground.

Devin laughed. "You ain't used to this heat, huh?"

I shook my head, because I couldn't speak. No wonder he
doesn't look biracial. The Phoenix sun fried him to golden perfec-
tion.

Devin looked at me like I was in another body. He smiled anxiously like a kid who'd just kissed his first girlfriend. The charming
young nineteen-year-old that I fell in love with reincarnated.

With about as much excitement as having bread and water for a
snack, he said, "Oh, my mom is having dinner for us tonight."

"That should be cool."

"I'm glad you think so."

He went on to warn me about his parents' expectations and pet peeves. "But don't let them agitate you. They're just a little uptight."

Irritated by his constant warning, I agreed, "Okay, Devin. I know."

We drove along a secluded road, which was parallel to a beautiful mountain called Camelback Mountain. Finally, we turned into a gated driveway. Devin pressed a button near his sunroof, and the gates opened. The driveway extended for about a half of a mile. A house seemed to miraculously appear. The sun setting behind the huge beige stucco house made it look like an oil painting. Beautifully molded windowpanes accentuated the mansion. My facial expression was probably screaming, "Wow!"

Instead of waiting for Devin to open my door, I jumped out. He grabbed my luggage from the trunk, and we headed for the huge wooden French doors. Devin clicked a button on his key, and the doors unlocked. I took one step into the home and almost fainted. The entire floor was crème marble. Beautiful artwork and sculptures were meticulously arranged in the foyer. Suddenly, Mrs. Patterson appeared from the sunroom on the left.

She artificially hugged me. "Clark, I'm glad you could finally make it out to see us. I thought you'd never visit."

It was plainly visible that she struggled to be polite. Her makeup was caked on just as I remembered. Her big blue eyes were lined with brown liner and brown mascara. She wore a white sleeveless sweater and black slacks that appeared to be custom fitted. How could her cooking possibly be tasty if she's flawless?

After attempting to extinguish any negativity that lingered in my head, I said, "Mrs. Patterson, I am really glad to be here. You have a lovely home."

"Thank you, sweetheart. Just make yourself comfortable."

Mrs. Patterson motioned for me to come along with her. We walked through a huge, elegant living room and up two steps into a beautiful loft. The room had an Aztec décor with washed wood furniture.

Mrs. Patterson gave me a summary of where to find anything in the room. After completing her evidently rehearsed overview, she concluded, "This is all yours for the weekend. I'll also show you Devin's place, because I'm sure you'll be spending time there as well." She gave me a conniving smirk like she didn't want me chilling with her son.

Devin seemed to have disappeared. How could he leave me alone with this woman? My mouth was dry as the Sahara Desert.

We walked in silence out of a sliding glass door, past the pool, and into the pool house. Devin's pad was actually the size of my one-bedroom apartment. She gave me a shabby tour of the pool house, practically telling me that she hoped I'd have limited exposure.

Devin opened the door to the pool house, munching on a small turkey croissant sandwich. I wanted to tackle him.

"Mom, why don't you let me finish giving Clark the tour and you go help Consuela get dinner together?"

I looked at Devin as if to say, "Who is Consuela?" He gave me an embarrassed grin. "She's the cook."

A damn cook. How did he disguise himself as normal? Trying to clear my mind of the fact that my man was an impersonator, I said, "I hope Consuela can cook, because I'm starving."

Just as I turned to look at Mrs. Patterson, I noticed an expression of disapproval on her face. I smiled to soften the atmosphere. She pursed her lips, raised her eyebrow, and pulled her neck back in an irritated manner, and said, "Well, I guess I will help Consuela. We have a hungry guest."

Just as fast as she made her sly comment, she tossed her hair back and exited the room. Was my comment inappropriate?

Devin walked over and rubbed my shoulders. "Baby, why do you look like that?" He wrapped his arms around me.

In a spoiled brat tone, I said, "I'm fine."

He lifted my chin. "Did she say something to upset you?"

"It's not what she says. It's how she says it." I shook my head, not wanting to believe that after all I've accomplished, I still come across as a poor little black girl from the ghetto. "You know, let's forget about this and I'll ignore everything like you said. Okay?"

He kissed me and said, "You know I wasn't planning on taking you on a tour."

He pushed his midsection close to mine. Unsure of how much privacy we had, I asked, "What about your mother?"

He kidded, "She doesn't play with me."

It was rather awkward making love and wondering if someone would catch us. We were both too apprehensive to enjoy it. A high school quickie was all I got after three weeks.

Devin's mother buzzed for us to come to dinner. We walked into the main house from a sliding glass door off of the kitchen. Every appliance in the kitchen was chrome. The cabinets were cherry, and the refrigerator was camouflaged with cherry wood panels. The island was loaded with food. Was someone else coming for dinner?

Devin proceeded to introduce me to Consuela. "Ms. Consuela, this is my Clark."

She grabbed me and gave me a warm motherly hug. The type I only wished Mrs. Patterson was capable of offering. Ms. Consuela was a middle-aged, overweight Mexican lady, with long brown hair.

With a deep Mexican accent, she said, "Clark, Devin talked my ear away about you all summer. I'm so glad you here. Now he can give me a break."

She laughed heartily and tagged Devin in the chest.

Devin kissed her on the cheek and wrapped his arm around her shoulder. "Yeah, we rap. Ms. Consuela is my dawg."

She gave him an artificially stern look. "I tell you about callin' me that."

We all laughed. As to interrupt our joyous moment, the warden marched in. "What are you all doing? Your father is seated at the table."

She walked away and gave Ms. Consuela a look that said, "Get moving."

It was strange because Devin seemed to relate to Consuela much better than he did to his own mother. Why hadn't Devin ever mentioned Consuela? They were obviously close. It concerned me that he could be deceptive enough to keep so many facets of his real life secret. Would the real Devin Patterson please stand up?

Devin grabbed my hand and led me into the dining room. I sluggishly followed. I much preferred to serve dinner with Consuela.

When we walked into the formal twenty-chair dining room, Mr. Patterson rose from his seat at the head of the table. With the most agitating Corporate American imitation, he said, "Hello, Clark. So, you've finally gotten the opportunity to come out and visit."

He extended his arm to shake my hand. The salads were already on the table. Waiting for someone to say grace, I sat patiently, but everyone began eating without giving God a moment of thanks. Did he even have a different relationship with God when he was around his parents?

I bowed my head and said my own private blessing. When I looked up, Mrs. Patterson stared in my face. I cracked a tense smile. Without acknowledging my peaceful gesture, she turned her head away to face her husband.

"Honey, Clark works for MICROS."

He said, "Really? We just represented Micros in an Intellectual Property case."

Mrs. Patterson confirmed, "Yes, they're the company that makes cash registers."

Mr. Patterson nodded. She'd practically degraded my job to make it sound like I worked on an assembly line.

I strained another fake smile. "Really?"

Mrs. Patterson frowned slightly and said. "Yes, really."

I planned to keep my mouth shut. Mr. Patterson tried to offset her ignorance. "So, Clark. What do you do at MICROS?"

"I'm a software engineer."

He nodded, seemingly granting his approval. "I could have used you yesterday. My computer in the office crashed."

Did I say I fixed computers? I'm an engineer, a professional. I smiled. "Really?"

The warden jumped in, "Are you originally from Maryland?"

"Yes, ma'am."

She turned her face up. "Please don't call me that. It makes me feel so old." Her snobbish laugh echoed in the room.

"I'm sorry. And yes, I am originally from Maryland."

She leaned toward me. "Do you plan on staying in Maryland?"

Devin and I have plans. Did she not know about them? I was afraid to ask.

I raised my shoulders. "Um, I don't know."

Like she was speaking to a complete jerk, she shook her head. "Well, I guess you are if you don't know. You have to start exploring your future plans."

How could she skillfully make a completely intelligent individual feel stupid? My heart started beating rapidly, fearing her next question.

Mr. Patterson said, "Honey, you have plenty of time."

She chewed her food and swallowed hard. "I guess. So, do you have other siblings in Maryland?"

Proudly, I sat up straight. "Yes, I have a brother, but he lives in New York. He's a stockbroker."

She covered her forehead. "Oh, no, not one of them."

She attempted to discredit the one person I am most proud of. I mumbled, "Yeah, he's one of them."

Then, as to deny the insult, she waved her hand. "Not that there's anything wrong with them. My broker recently made some bad decisions. Now I have it out for all of them."

She began her witchlike laughter again. I reluctantly chuckled.

"So, does he have a family in New York?"

I breathed heavily, certain that I could never explain that he has two kids in Maryland. "No."

Mr. Patterson said, "That's nice. So, just the two of you. Your parents must be really proud."

I nodded. "Yes, my mother is very proud of us."

Mrs. Patterson slyly asked, "And your father, do you know him?"

To confirm her negative assumption, I sassily said, "Nope."

She pulled her neck back and batted her eyelashes. She and Mr. Patterson exchanged silent conversation. When I stared at him, he pretended to clear his thought. With artificial compassion, he said, "That's unfortunate."

"Yep. He was killed by a racist cop when I was seven."

I laughed quietly to myself. They both looked embarrassed.

Thankfully, Ms. Consuela walked in with dessert. Dead air as I fumbled over the apple pie. I studied Devin, who'd looked at his plate through the entire meal. Why didn't he jump in to save me from their attacks?

I promised never to return to the Pattersons' again. Despite my love for Devin, I could never survive visiting his parents.

After Devin and I were excused from the grand table, we headed for the pool house. Near the pool, Devin stopped and wrapped his arm around my shoulder and pulled me to him. With my head buried in his chest, I began to cry. He said, "Clark, she's demeaning. I know. I don't know why I asked you to come out here."

I looked above, searching for a lucky star. A moon half the size of the sky glared into my watery eyes. I began to speak, "Devin, I'm a big girl. I'm not crying because they hurt my feelings. I'm crying because I feel like I have to suppress who I am to appear worthy to them."

He tried to interject, "But—"

"Devin, you don't have to apologize for them. Or me, for that matter."

"What are you saying?"

I asked, "Devin, do I embarrass you? Why did you hide me for so long?"

"Clark, I was hiding them. They're the assholes."

"Go ahead, tell me. Tell me the truth. You don't think I'm good enough. Do you?"

I covered my face with my hands, trying to erase the vision of his graduation. "I'm not the perfect little girl that your family raised you to be with. Am I? I'm just a little hood rat."

Words I've never uttered to anyone, but thoughts that haunted me spilled from my mouth.

"No college degree, no amount of success, will erase what you and your parents see. A poor little hood rat. Right, Devin! Right?"

"Clark, you're trippin'! Every time I turn around you're huffing and puffing about something. I'm tired of pacifying your insecurities. I don't believe you just said all that soap-opera bullshit."

The little ghetto girl that I tried so hard to stifle appeared from her hiding place. "What the fuck do you mean? I'm trippin'. You're trippin'." I got in his face. "Who are you, anyway?"

Devin put his head down and walked to the pool house. I followed, still awaiting answers. When I walked through the sliding glass door, Devin sat on the pastel wicker couch with his head inside of his hands.

I stood directly in front of him and pointed my finger like it was a loaded gun. "Tell me that! Who are you?"

Surprisingly, he looked at me. "This is me. I'm tired of pretending." He opened his arms. "This is me."

I pleaded, "But why do you change when you get around them?"

Appearing fed up with his charade, he admitted, "I change when I'm around you. This is where I was raised. This is who I am. Maybe that makes me uptight, too. Like you always say, you hate uptight people. I guess you hate me, too."

"Those are your words. You didn't introduce me to your family for years, because you said they were uptight. I'm using your words. Or the words of the man that I'm in love with, because you damn sure ain't him."

"Clark, what the fuck ever."

His attitude said I could end the debate. I shut up and walked into Devin's bedroom, where I fell asleep. Awakened by Devin's instrument separating my thighs, my arteries pumped with skepticism. I refused to subject myself to sleeping with a stranger. Softly, I whispered, "Stop. I don't want to."

He continued to force himself into my entrance. I screamed, "Stop!"

Apparently the words were not audible, because he handled his business. His thrusts were fast and hard in a violent manner. I stopped moving. His brutal aggression was so intense that the heavy bed moved around. Petrified, I began to cry. He put his head into the pillow, his cheek next to mine. The moistness on my face rubbed against his. He raised his head and grabbed my hair. "What's wrong now?"

"Devin, just get off of me!"

"After I come!" He yanked my hair harder, like he was trying to pull it from the roots.

He overpowered me as I tried to push him away. Unmercifully, I was forced to endure his cruel abuse until he was satisfied. He stared at me like a crazed animal, as he squirted his fluid all over my stomach and thighs. He rolled onto his back and immediately began to snore. I sat up in the bed to look at the man who had violated me. What had taken over him? Was he possessed by a demon? I slid out of the bed, as not to awaken the vampire. He didn't move. My hot spot burned with abrasive irritation.

The lights were still on when I walked out of the room. Two empty bottles of Hennessy sat on the coffee table. Devin was drunk. Not that it was a viable excuse, but for me, it explained his hostile act.

When I got back into the main house, I lay in the bed for a moment with my clothes on. Then I forced myself to get in the shower to wash away the evil spirit that he put on me. The rage on Devin's face while he viciously attacked me kept me awake. I was definitely in love with two different men.

I caught the earliest flight back to Baltimore in the morning and promised never to look back.

25

DEVIN

When I woke up, Clark was gone. She had called a taxi and left. She told my mother there was an emergency at home. I remembered arguing with her. I tried to make up, but she didn't give in.

After accepting that she was really gone, I showered. I had planned to take Clark to the mountains, so my schedule was empty. I lounged around in bed, hoping Clark would call to say she made it home safely. Then again, I didn't know if I wanted to see her silly ass again. One minute I thought she was the girl out of my dreams. The next minute, I couldn't even stand the sound of her scratchy voice.

I picked up the phone and dialed my study partner, Jennifer. It was time to act on my year-long crush.

She picked up the phone. "Hello . . ."

How sweet the sound of a peaceful woman?

"Hey, Jay. It's me, Devin."

I could see the smile stretched across her face.

"Devin? Hey!"

I was prepared to bust a move. Hustling past the small talk, "I miss you, girl."

"You know what, Devin? I miss you, too."

Trying to flatter myself, I pushed for assurance. "I don't believe you. Why haven't you called me, then?"

"Honestly, I felt like you may have changed your mind and stayed in Maryland with your girlfriend."

Confirming the end of my relationship, I proceeded to tell Jennifer how I felt about Clark. "Man, we broke up. I got tired of the drama. I'm too young to deal with it."

Hesitantly, she responded, "Well, if you're happy, I'm happy for you. When are you coming back to New York?"

I said, "Whenever you tell me you want me to come back."

"I wanted you back the minute you left."

Ms. Jennifer had obviously waited all year to hear me say it was over with Clark. Her response shocked me. She was always so composed whenever I attempted to flirt. She bit the hell out of my bait.

"Why didn't you say something, then?"

"I didn't know what you would think of me."

"You shouldn't have worried about that. Life is too short to worry about what people think of you."

"Well, I'm sorry, but I do care what you think of me."

"Why is that?"

Jennifer totally ignored my question. She made a comment about something that she was watching on television.

After an overly flirtatious conversation with Jennifer, I erased the thought of calling Clark. It was time to move on and let go. The Clark that I wanted to marry had disappeared a long time ago. We were both holding on to strangers. She claimed that she didn't know me, and I damn sure didn't know her anymore.

26

CLARK

The moment I stepped in the door from the airport, I dodged for my nightstand. I rummaged through the junk to find Troy's phone number. I immediately dialed the number, hoping he could help me get my mind off of Devin.

His voice mail came on. I left my name and number, uncertain of what to expect.

In ten minutes flat, my phone rang. I quickly picked up. "Hello."

"Hi, can I speak with Clark please?"

"This is Clark."

"Clark, this is Troy."

"Hi, Troy. I've been so busy."

He cut into my explanation. "Don't even worry about it. I told you I was patient, right?"

"Yeah."

"So, are you trying to go out tonight?"

My eyelids were down to my cheeks. My mind wanted to go, but my body was just too tired. "No, but we can do something to-morrow if you want."

"Tomorrow I'm going to Myrtle Beach with my friends."

"How long are you going to be there?"

"Seven days."

Tired and disappointed, I sighed. "Well, I guess I'll see you when you get back."

"Or we could do something relaxing tonight."

I contemplated. "Like what?"

"Where do you stay?"

"In Columbia."

"Let's go out to the lake and talk. I promise, I'll have you home and in bed by eleven."

He lied. We sat out on the lake until three in the morning. We talked about his multiple relationships. I talked about my dysfunctional relationship. Both of us in need of counseling, but the other sufficed.

I woke up, thinking about Troy, angry about Devin. He didn't call to see if I'd made it home safely or if everyone in my family was okay. He didn't care.

The moment I turned my ringer on, the phone rang. "Hello."

"Hey, Clark. It's Troy."

His voice was so soothing, so relaxed. "Good morning."

I yawned. "What's up? Are you on the road yet?"

"Not yet. I had such a good time talking to you last night. I've never met a female that I felt comfortable telling everything to."

"Yeah, I enjoyed your company, too."

"I don't know if I wanna put you on little sister status or what."

Not wanting to destroy the possibilities, I said, "I already have a big brother."

He laughed. "I hear you."

"I hope so."

"Well, Clark, I need to get ready to hit the road. I'll call you when I get there."

He called every day. Often, he called twice a day. Devin didn't bother. My heart ached, and I shared it freely with Troy.

27

DEVIN

After I spoke to Jennifer, I couldn't get to New York fast enough. Jennifer met me at the airport. When I walked out of the terminal, she stood up and glided so gracefully toward me. She wore a pair of skin-tight white stretch denim shorts that barely covered her butt cheeks and a white tank top that clearly exposed her bare nipples. Her lips felt like menthol invigorating my skin when she pecked me on the cheek. I planned to make that casual gesture a thing of the past. When I hugged her, I massaged her back like she was my lady. I grabbed her butt in my hands and pretended that I was pulling her shorts down. Surprisingly, she just continued holding me, as if it was okay for me to strip her naked in the airport. That turned me on. I cut the hug short, because I was ready to dive into Jennifer. From her body language, Jennifer was willing to let me swim freely.

We grabbed a bite to eat at the airport and headed straight to my apartment. Jennifer helped me bring the luggage up to my apartment. She was anxious to get the show rolling as well. Jennifer hadn't had sex in over two years. It made me horny just imagining that I'd be like the first man ever to step foot in the place.

Once everything was in the apartment, I wrapped my arms around Jennifer's waist and backed her up to my bedroom. She graciously rubbed the back of my head as she backed up. It was written all over her face; she wanted Mr. Big Stuff badly. I picked her up and laid her on my bed. I stood on the side of the bed to admire her body. Jennifer appeared uncomfortable with the observance. She kicked her mules off and scooted back nervously. I smiled to lighten up the moment. She retorted with an uneasy smirk.

Just to confirm, I asked, "Are you sure this is what you want?"

She nodded. No turning back. I started at her feet and planned to work my way over every inch of her body. I landed moist kisses on her feet. She wiggled. I raised her leg and kissed her inner thigh. As I stroked her leg with my tongue, I slowly removed her shorts. Then I put my mouth on her sunshine and let it beam on me. She proclaimed her pleasure with soothing sighs and moans. Once she was full with desire, I grabbed the condom from my pocket and rapidly prepared for feeding. Excitedly, I plunged inside. Everything I imagined. Warm and tight like a virgin.

Jennifer made the sweetest expressions, so gentle, so delicate. She massaged my ego with every *ooh* and thrilled my manhood with every *ah*. As I reached my peak, I made muffled moans. How can I be tossed in one session? Once we arrived, total satisfaction escaped our bodies, through heavy breathing. My nature softened inside of her. I couldn't move. She was lethal. She stung me. My limbs were paralyzed. She spoke, breaking the innocent silence. "Devin, I hope you really left your girl . . ."

I swear. She really fucked up a perfectly lovely experience. That was the last thing that I expected to discuss. How does she plan to keep me happy? She had the initial code to my happiness, good sex. I want to get inside of her head to see if she can sustain it. I want to find all of the cobwebs and scars that were left by the previous owner. Then I will know if Jennifer is going to make it to "girlfriend" status. Casual relationships don't thrill me. I like to know if someone is worth my full time loving. If not, it's time for me to move on and find my queen. I thought Clark was the answer. It took me over three years to notice the baggage she carried. Then again, she stored it extremely well. With Jennifer, I wanted to take my time before I planned forever.

After I didn't entertain her question, she spoke softly while sliding from beneath my body. "Just don't hurt me . . ."

I rose up on my side and looked at Jennifer, lying on her back with her forearm draped over her forehead, as to question her actions. I put my chin on her shoulder and began to kiss her jaw line. Then I said, "Jennifer, I don't play games with women. It's not my style. I wouldn't lie to you just to get in your pants. I respect you too much for that." Still kissing her soft face, I waited for her approval. "Okay?"

Seemingly relaxed, she wrapped her arm around my back and began to caress it. She nodded, acknowledging her faith in me.

28

CLARK

After no word from Devin in eight weeks, the relationship was obviously over. Yet, I still awaited his call. I still awaited his apology. Troy took me to nice places, bought me nice things, but Devin filled my mind. Whenever Troy got a few steps closer, I pulled back. In order to move on, I had to speak to Devin.

I picked up the phone and called Devin in New York. While dialing the numbers, questions haunted me, but I continued. I refused to let my pride interfere with my peace. The phone rang three times. Assuming he was looking at the caller ID and intentionally avoiding my call, I started to hang up. Just then, someone picked up. "Hello."

A female's voice traveled through the line. My heart dropped. Before I spoke, I thought positively. Maybe Devin had changed his number. I said, "I'm sorry, I was trying to reach Devin Patterson, and . . ."

"Oh, he's asleep right now, but . . . can I take a message?"

My bladder released, right there on my bed. I soaked my mattress. After I picked my lip up from the floor, I said, "Um . . ." Trying to find the right words, "Uh . . ."

"Miss . . . do you wanna leave a message?"

Inflicted with a speech impediment, "Uuuuh . . . yeeeeah."

Slowly rolling my heavy tongue, I searched for the words to handle this unanticipated situation. Impatient breathing on the other end confused me more. In just two months, another victim, poisoned and immobilized by Devin's love. From her sigh, the last thing she expected was a speechless female on the other end. I thought back to how I fell in love with Devin in just one short week. Something told me that this girl probably felt the same. Mr. Hyde had struck again.

I didn't know how to proceed, but as far as I was concerned, Devin still owed me respect. "This is Clark."

I paused, hoping to hear intimidation in her breathing. After concluding that my name didn't strike an explicit reaction, I proceeded, "I need you to wake him up."

"Why? Is there a problem?"

Oh, this hooker really wants to see me act ugly. I sat up in my bed, as to prepare for verbal war. "Yes, I would like to know who's answering his phone . . . and . . ."

Before I could complete my sentence, she said, "Clark, this is Jennifer. Now you know who's answering his phone."

Remembering that she was just his study partner that I'd heard all about, I felt relieved. Uncertain if things had progressed, I queried, "Oh, you're Devin's study partner."

"And his lover."

What the hell? I couldn't believe my ears. "His what?"

As smooth as Hennessy straight, she said, "I'm sure you heard me. You just don't want to believe it. Try back later. Devin should be up, and he'll tell you himself."

Then she pleasantly hung up the phone. My heart was shattered glass. In less than eight weeks, this bastard had a bitch answering his phone.

Little Ms. Study Partner was probably the splinter in my finger the entire first year. Who knew? There was no need for further speculation.

How can I digest all of this at once? Not only had he not called, but he was in another relationship.

Finally, I stood up and removed my wet bed sheets. I turned the shower on and began removing my clothes. Just as I was about to step in the shower, the phone rang. Oh, God, what would I say? He probably cursed Jennifer out and ran for the phone.

I rushed to the phone. "Hello."

"Hey, girl. Whatcha doing?" It was Tanisha.

"Hey."

"Damn. You sound like I'm the last person you wanna talk to." She continued, "For real. What's wrong with you?"

"The same thing that's been wrong."

"Clark." She sighed, like she would relieve my pain if she could.

"I know. I should be over it. But today, I . . ."

"You what?"

How do I explain? I wanted to lie, but there was nothing to lie about. He was a jerk, and I had to accept it.

All she could say was, "Damn, Clark."

"Tanisha, go ahead, tell me how much of an ass he is."

"Clark, I don't have to keep telling you that. It's not going to help. It will only make it hurt more. It's hard to get over someone you believe in. Shit, you know I've been there."

We both sighed, acknowledging the truth in her words. For me, it helped to know that through it all, she moved on.

29

DEVIN

Jennifer started to become overwhelming. All day, every day, she wanted to fuck. I pretended to be totally exhausted and slipped into a well-deserved anesthetic sleep. While I slept, I dreamed of my Clark. So much of being with Jennifer left me longing for my baby. The Clark that I fell in love with, the one who used to entertain me, so free and fun-loving.

When I woke up, I went straight for the shower. Jennifer practically tackled me, wanting to know if she could shower with me. Shit. I missed Clark's smoothness. Jennifer was like a python around my neck. I stopped her. "Babe, give me a little me time."

She looked offended. She puckered her small lips. "Why?"

"I just wanna chill for a second and do some thinking."

Smiling, like she thought I'd tell her, "And what are you thinking?"

"Thinking about how happy you make me."

I lied. How could I tell her what I was truly thinking? She smiled gently, this trusting smile, like she was handing me her heart in a gift-wrapped box.

I slipped on a pair of sweats after I got out of the shower and stretched across the bed. Jennifer lay on the bed beside me and began caressing my chest slowly. She held her head up with her hand, leaning her elbow into the pillow. She stared at me, as if she was searching for the answers to a final exam. I wrapped my arm around her body and began stroking her back. I mumbled, "What's up?"

Hoping she'd say, "Nothing, baby." Instead she said, "Do you still love Clark?"

What the fuck? Jennifer had not mentioned Clark's name since I told her she was the one for me. Did something on my face show that I missed Clark more and more each day? I tried to remain cool. Still in the same calm tone, I asked, "What made you ask me that?"

My heart raced. Jennifer smiled a conniving grin and said, "I just need to know. Don't you think that I deserve to know?"

I shrugged my shoulders. We could hear a feather drop.

Finally, she mumbled something and sat up on the side of the bed and sipped her drink. She said something about Clark that I couldn't decipher. Then she said it again. This time, loud enough for me to hear. "Clark called you."

I was ecstatic. We still had it, our subliminal connection. My dick almost got hard. Before my excitement showed in my actions, I calmly asked, "When? What did she say?"

Jennifer threw the contents in her glass at me. Dark acidic liquid dripped from my confused face. I grabbed Jennifer and held her in my arms. She didn't ask to be there. I told her that it was over, and God only knew what Clark said to her. How did I put my friend in this situation? I wasn't away from Clark for twenty-four hours before I started entertaining jumping into the sack with Jennifer. My dick guided me straight into her and shot an arrow through her vulnerable heart.

As I held her, I could feel her heart beating feverishly. A few tears rolled from her eyes. "Why did you look so happy when I said she called?"

Misleading Jennifer any longer would only cause her more pain. With every intention to be honest, I spoke, "I don't know. I really don't know. All I know is that everything I've told you was true."

She yanked away from me and plopped on the bed. "What the fuck are you saying?"

I stood in front of her and stared deep in her eyes. "What I am saying is that I have not spoken with Clark since I told you it was over, and I . . ."

I paused. I didn't know what else to say. That was all there was to it. She interrupted my moment of silence. "And, what?"

"And I swear, I haven't thought about her since I've been with you." Shit, I'd lied before I even realized what I was saying. The weakness in her eyes scared me.

Jennifer wiped the tears streaming down her face. "You know what, Devin, maybe you should take a couple of days to be alone. Then tell me you haven't thought about her. I've just served as a distraction. You don't know how you feel about her. You haven't had time to think about it. I'm just sorry that I was stupid enough to let you use me for a rebound."

"Baby, naw, you're not a rebound. I really care about you."

She stood up and put her hand over my mouth. In control of her rage, she spoke calmly. "I know. Really, I do. I know that you care about me, but you still care about her and you need to get in touch with your feelings."

Though I wanted her to lighten up, it crushed me that she was the one taking the initiative to leave. Suddenly, I desperately needed her. "Naw, Jennifer . . . baby, I need you. I don't need time."

She was so tranquil. "Devin, I'm not going anywhere. I just want you to take a few days and think about what you want. You don't know. Trust me. I've been through what you're going through."

She nonchalantly walked into the other room to grab her backpack and shoes. Waddling behind her like a small puppy, I asked her to stay. Before I realized it, Jennifer turned the doorknob. I walked over and gave her a kiss on the cheek.

"I'm sorry. I don't want us to go through this."

"Devin, it's life. You have feelings."

She was entirely too damn understanding. It was downright horrifying. "Thanks for being cool."

Ironically, she gave me her special smile and said, "You have changed my life, and I love you despite your decision."

Like that, she was gone. I took a second to regroup before dialing Clark's number.

When the phone rang, I suddenly became nervous. As if she was awaiting my call, she answered on the first ring. "Hey."

Hey is her way of saying, "What Nigga?" Shit, I was thinking, "Hell, I heard you called me."

Instead, I approached the situation like a man. I should have been the one to call her a long time ago. "Hello, Clark. How are you?"

Clark evaded the formalities. "I'm wondering how the fuck, we've been apart for a hot minute and you have a bitch answering the phone, talking 'bout she's your lover . . . that's how I'm doing."

Whoa. My game plan was tossed off course. My only recourse was to apologize to Clark for everything. I would have blown Maryland up if I called her and a dude picked up the phone. "Baby . . ."

Before I could start, "I'm not your fucking baby . . ."

"Clark, let me finish. I'm sorry. I swear I'm so sorry for everything I've done to you."

Hearing her sniffle made me long to ease her pain. I continued with my testimony. "Baby, I admit I've jumped into something on the rebound." As I spoke the words, I accepted the reality of what I was doing to Jennifer. "But, there hasn't been a day that I haven't pictured your smile, heard your silly giggle, dreamed about the times when we lived each day for what it was worth."

She sighed. She could relate to me. I wanted to keep her on the same page with me. "You remember that? Huh?"

She was literally crying at this point. "Yeah, man. I remember. What happened? Where did it all go wrong?"

"We stopped appreciating the 'what is' in life. We started living for the 'what's going to be.' The present is a reality, and the future is just a possibility. That's where we went wrong."

She laughed. I mean, she giggled. My stomach rumbled with joy to hear my baby girl happy again. She kidded me with her impression of the secretary on the *Steve Harvey Show*. "You right, you right, Mr. Smart Man."

She changed her tone to a more serious one. "Honestly, though, Devin, do you think that was the real problem?"

"No, that wasn't entirely the reason. I fucked up . . . a lot. In living for the day, I kept things from you, and things haven't been totally right since you thought I was hiding you. And honestly, it wasn't intentional. I was young and immature. I took a sorry-ass approach."

For the first time, I admitted to Clark the real reason why things erupted. She'd trusted me with all her heart, and I'd withheld crucial information from her for no reason at all. After that, things never got back to normal. Obviously, life's circumstances took some effect on the relationship, but my useless lie or lack of truth about my heritage was the initial crack in our shattered relationship. She was afraid to trust me after that.

"You know, Devin. I'm sorry you took that approach, too. I believed in you. I thought you were the strongest, most intelligent man on earth. Then to find out that you were a coward. That hurt like hell. I tried to let it go, but you were conniving enough to hide me, a woman you were planning to marry." She took a breath. "I mean, I don't know. I love you so much. I just wish I believed in you like I did before."

Damn, she really hit home. I couldn't say anything about it. I received those words and meditated on them. She couldn't have said it better. She waited for a response. I sighed and said, "I'm sorry, baby. I didn't mean to hurt you."

"Devin, I know that. That's the only reason I'm talking to you now. I know you aren't a bad person. I made some wrong choices, too. I should have moved to New York, but I was too afraid to put my world into your hands. I didn't want you to drop me. I mean, we both made bad decisions, but your last one was . . ."

She sighed as if the thought was too painful. Certain it was in reference to the weekend in Phoenix, I began, "For real, Clark, I don't even know what happened. When I woke up, you were gone, and I felt like you chose not to accept my family. And like I said then, I am a part of them. So, if we're going to be together, you'll have to accept them or ignore them."

"I respect that, but that's not what I'm talking about. You sexually abused me."

I laughed. She continued to tell me how much of an asshole I was that night. Never move on to a new relationship before you verbally settle the score in an old one. I'd thought that she was the asshole, and all the while it was me.

Clark and I talked on the phone for the next three hours. Without truly saying that we were back together, we were happy because the war had ceased.

30

CLARK

I slept peacefully. The morning sun greeted me. The sound of Tina Marie's voice filled my apartment. Singing along as I prepared for work, "I'm out on the limb. I'm giving in to you again . . ." Pride in my voice, happy to give in to the man of my life.

Just as I was about to hop in the shower, my phone rang. I ran into the bedroom and grabbed the receiver without looking at my caller ID. "Hello."

"Baby."

"Yes, Devin."

"I just called to tell you that I am so sorry for being such an asshole. I couldn't sleep last night, thinking about how I made you feel when you were in Phoenix."

I didn't want to stir up those negative visions again. "Devin, I know you're sorry. Honestly, I'm okay. Let's forget about that. Let it go." Coaxing him into saying what I wanted to hear, "I thought you were calling to say you loved me."

"Oh, no doubt! I love you to death."

When we hung up the night before, we felt awkward. Neither of us said those endearing words. Like new lovers still fearing that if we revealed our feelings, we would appear vulnerable. It shocked me to hear him say it without fear or hesitation. I reciprocated his sincerity. "I love you, too. And I miss you. How about that?"

"I'm going to make a trip to see you this weekend."

I wanted to catch the next Express Jet to New York. This weekend seemed like a long time to wait. His voice triggered excitement in every erotic zone in my body. I couldn't imagine waiting four days. As my mind wandered into the world of expediting my encounter with Devin, I realized that I couldn't just go to New York anymore. Devin needed to exterminate the pests first.

I walked into work feeling refreshed and renewed. I sat at my desk for about an hour, browsing through e-mail and scribbling Devin's name on my sticky pad. Back in love and I hadn't even seen the man. How could I be sure that his words were genuine without looking into his eyes?

After I daydreamed for most of the day, I finally decided that it was time to feed my tummy. Just as I grabbed my purse, my phone rang.

"Micros, Clark speaking . . ."

"What would you give to see your man right now?"

Shit! I would give anything. Trying to remain cool, "I'll tell you if you tell me how soon my man can get here."

He laughed. "Baby, I'm sitting outside of your apartment. Tell me how soon you can get here."

Devin was probably quite surprised when he tried the door. I'd changed the locks when I came from Phoenix.

"Ten minutes . . . I'll be there. Don't go anywhere!"

I shut down my workstation and scurried out of the office. I ducked and dodged traffic in my desperate pursuit to see my man. The thought only caused me to drive faster.

When I pulled up into the complex, my stomach felt unsettled. Devin sat in his car, parked about three spaces from the building.

I slowly stepped one foot out of my car and pushed my hair behind my ear. Afraid to approach the man I've known forever, I glanced in my rearview mirror. Before I could shut the door, Devin was out of his car and walking toward me. Nervously, I smiled as he reached out to hug me. I mumbled, "Hey, baby."

"Hey." He pulled me closer and squeezed me tightly. "Damn, you feel so good. I missed you."

I was baffled. I wanted him and I needed him, but I was unsure about his motives. He seemed so anxious to be there, but he had a girl that he was sleeping with in New York. If he missed me so much, why did I have to initiate communication?

I returned his affection by landing kisses along his neck. "Baby, I missed you, too."

Just as I spoke the truth, my eyes watered. I pulled back. I wanted to look into his eyes, and I needed him to see the pain in mine.

He wiped my eyes and put his right arm around me, directing me to turn around. We headed toward the building. I tried to break the ice. "Damn, baby. Did you even take a shower this morning? You look like you just hopped out of bed."

He laughed. "I did. After I hung up, I contemplated if I should come or not. Then I said, 'Fuck it,' put on some sweats, and got on the road."

"Are you serious?"

"What do you think?"

When I opened the door of my apartment, I felt embarrassed. The place was a wreck and my room even worse.

"Damn, girl. Did a tornado hit this place?"

I played on his pity. "Naw, just a broken heart."

He sighed. "Damn, baby. I'm sorry."

Since he caused it, I decided to make him suffer with every opportunity. He lounged on the couch. Still a little apprehensive, I paced the floor. I looked over at his sexy body stretched across my couch, and I wanted to lie with him. Instead, I started straightening the room. Conscious of every step, I searched for words to keep the atmosphere relaxed. Devin noticed my preoccupation.

"Clark, why are you doing busy work? Just chill with your man. Damn."

He sat up and opened his arms, inviting me to be held. I felt clumsy walking to him. Finally, after what seemed like a walk across country, I stood in front of Devin, my stomach at his head. My arms wrapped around his neck as he rested his head on my stomach. I swayed to avoid just being in the moment. He aggressively grabbed my hips and held them still.

"Clark, why are you acting like you're scared of your man?"

"Devin, how are you my man when you're sleeping with Jennifer?"

He removed his hands from around my waist and sat back. He shook his head. And the bastard said, "I don't know . . ."

Stunned by his response, I stumbled backward. Why didn't he just say he told Jennifer that it was over? I slipped into the chair across from him. What's left to say?

I sat there, waiting for the words. Still nothing. Finally, Devin said, "Baby, it's going to be hard."

"What? To leave her . . ."

He smiled. "Let me finish. It's going to be hard to get over this, but we can. When I get back to New York, I'll tell Jennifer. I'm not trying to lose you. After all this time, we still have it. I can't lose that for anything. I mean that shit, Clark."

Not even his parents? I asked the next most important thing on my mind. "So, how could you move on without calling me? Why did I have to call you first?"

"Clark, I don't know. When I found out that you called, I was happy as shit. I even questioned myself. How the hell could I be in pain and not be man enough to call. I still don't have the answer. That's crazy, isn't it?"

"No, it's a crying shame." We both laughed.

Jennifer answering his phone still aggravated me. It made me feel like she had taken my place, but Devin's eyes told me that he loved me and only me.

As I came to peace with reality, my body relaxed. Devin turned the TV on.

"Baby, if you don't have any more questions, can you come lay with me?"

Awaiting his request, I said, "Let's go in the bedroom."

Still looking at the TV, he said, "I'm right behind you."

I pushed as much junk as I could in the closet before Devin saw it. I turned the ringer off. I removed my clothes. When Devin walked in, I was wearing my bra and panties. His face flustered as he admired my body.

I put my hand on my hip, as to say, "So, what you gonna do with all this woman?"

He pulled me to him and held me. I could feel the firmness through his sweats. I reached in his pants and grabbed my friend. I stroked it. Harder and harder. The huge pipe filled to capacity. I needed it. I wanted it. When I pushed him on the bed, he pulled his sweats and boxers off in one swoop. Certain of my intentions, he smiled.

On my knees, I gazed at it, protruding from his body. My mouth covered it. Just the way he liked it, deep, slow, wet. Melting on my tongue, he exhaled pleasurable grunts. Satisfied that I could satisfy, I blushed.

"I love you. Damn, I love you."

When I stopped, he was prepared to love me. Right there on my bedroom floor, he laid me down. I whispered, "Get a condom."

He ignored me and slid into his perfectly heated pool without a cap on. So breathtaking, I failed to warn him again. My body responded pleasurably to the joy pervading inside. Slowly, softly he pleased me. Our bodies climaxed in harmony. His honey released with nothing to catch it. Sweetness filled me.

On top of me, he breathed heavily. I whispered in between gasps for air, "I love you, Devin."

"I love you, too."

We climbed our funky butts in the bed and fell asleep. For the remainder of the evening, over and over, totally natural passion was trapped inside my bedroom walls.

After intimacy restored my confidence, I asked, "Devin, where do we go from here?"

"This is where I want to be."

"So, what are you going to do about that freak, Jennifer?"

He chuckled. "I'm going to let it go."

"What do you think she'll say?"

Jokingly, he said, "She'll probably come get you . . ."

I tagged his chest. "Don't play. You know I'll beat her down."

"Yeah, I know."

Getting back on the topic at hand, "So, what are you going to tell her? Are you going to tell her we're back together?"

"Yes."

Trying to get all the necessary clauses in our verbal contract, I asked, "So, how are we going to do this?"

He bent over and kissed me. "By any means necessary."

Signed and notarized with his final words, the agreement was made. There was nothing left to do except believe in my man.

31

DEVIN

Our hearts beat at the same pace. I hadn't slept so peacefully since we'd been apart. Her body temperature warmed me like steam from a sauna. The sensual aroma of her body mesmerized me. When I touched her warm caramel skin, blood circulated freely through my body.

Conjuring up a way to explain to Jennifer in less than forty-eight hours that I was back in love with Clark seemed impossible. When she'd said take time, she'd wanted me to take a few days to get over Clark.

Clark moved around. I squeezed my eyes closed. She turned her body around to face me. She placed her arm around me. I could feel her staring at me like she longed to read my mind. In my attempt to play possum, she giggled.

"Stop faking! I see you blinking."

I laughed. She softly pushed my forehead with the palm of her hand and jumped out of bed.

As she headed to the bathroom for her early morning relief, she asked, "Bob Evans?"

"Yep."

I stood up and looked around the room. I spotted a pair of male shorts in a pile of clothes in the corner. It couldn't be possible. I picked them up. They weren't mine. My head began to throb. I yelled, "Hey, Clark!"

While brushing her teeth, she said, "What?"

I walked to the bathroom door holding the shorts by the gaudy leather belt. "Whose shorts are these?"

She rapidly rinsed her mouth out and said, "Yours or Reggie's."

Guilt glared in her eyes. She raised her shoulders like she was completely clueless.

I stood directly in front of her. I looked down at her. She looked up at me, seeking forgiveness. "You really want me to believe that these are Reggie's shorts?"

She wrapped her arms around me. "Devin, trust me, I haven't been with anyone."

Afraid to pry any further, I returned her affection. "I trust you, Clark. I trust you."

I got back to New York just in time to rush into my three o'clock class. With just a pen in my hand, I hurried in and found an empty desk.

Refusing to catch a glimpse of her innocent smile, I looked ahead for the entire class. My mind straight on my love life. Clark? Jennifer?

Each time I thought of staying with Jennifer, I repeated positive affirmations. "You have to be happy. You can't worry about anyone else."

When the instructor finished his lecture, anxiety numbed me. While others shuffled papers and packed bags, I sat there. Finally, I turned to find a missing Jennifer.

I rushed from the class. Maybe she exited from the rear door. I asked one of my classmates, had he seen her?

"Not in the last two days. Neither of you were in class yesterday."

Oh, no, had she gone and spent a day with an old boyfriend? Jealousy befuddled me.

I jogged out of the building toward Jennifer's apartment. It rapidly became a fast run like I was in a marathon. Thoughts, I mean, prayers circled through my head. "Please, God, don't let her be with another man."

Jennifer was too precious to be with anyone else. I couldn't bear the thought that hurt could send her flying into another man's arms. As I ran down Amsterdam Avenue, I wondered, What the hell I was thinking? For a man about to walk out of her life, I was fuming with jealousy, fear. Why did I care if she was with another man?

Sweat poured from my face; adrenaline rushed through my veins. Then as if I was struck by lightning, I stopped abruptly. Lost, caught in a love triangle, running from one woman's arms to the next. Who did I love? I really didn't know. I turned around and headed home.

Clark had asked me a question once. Can a man really love two women? At the time, I felt it was impossible. In the midst of it, there was no doubt. I love different things about each one.

With Clark there is this magnetic attraction; after four years I still find her irresistible. Jennifer, on the other hand, gives me something different, a safety net.

As I slowly turned to walk back to my car, I thought about the two women in my life. I thought about Jennifer's innocence. I thought about those denim shorts in Clark's room.

I heard Jennifer's soft voice. "Where you going?"

She walked toward me. Her slanted eyes were puffy and red like she sat up all night with tissues and the *Waiting to Exhale* CD. I couldn't bring myself to hurt her, not at that very moment.

"I was coming to see you, but I . . ."

"Why did you turn around?"

"'Cause I, um . . ." I couldn't think.

She ignored my stuttering. "C'mon, let's get some coffee."

I nodded without making eye contact. We headed over 113th Street to Starbucks on Broadway. When we walked into Starbucks, she asked, "What are you having?"

"Uh . . ." I couldn't even decide on a drink. "Uh, I mean, Café Mocha."

I handed her a ten-dollar bill and sat at the closest table. I stared out of the window, praying that Jennifer would tell me she didn't want me anymore.

Finally, the drinks were ready, and she walked over and took her seat.

"So, where did you go? Were you with her?"

Why did she have to be so blunt? The coffee cup that was heading toward my lip somehow tipped over right before its destination. Coffee dripped from my coat. I jumped up, shaking the liquid from my hands.

"Damn!"

I intentionally overdramatized the incident to evade the question. After grabbing a few napkins, I walked back to the table like a turtle.

The second I took my seat, she continued, "Where were you?"

I took a deep breath before I spoke. "I was with Clark."

"And you're not over her, are you?"

I could hear the pain in her voice. I couldn't hurt her more than what I already had, so I lied, "I don't know."

I looked down at my coffee when I spoke. When I looked up to see her reaction, her eyes were full.

Damn. What the hell was I supposed to do in the middle of Starbucks?

I grabbed her hand. "I'm sorry, Jay. I shouldn't have put you in the middle of this. I am so sorry."

She began to cry. "I know you didn't mean it, but I'm . . ." She paused, shook her head, like it was inexpressible. "I'm late."

"Naw, baby, it's not your fault."

She twisted her face. "Devin, what are you saying? I said, 'I'm late!'"

Suddenly, a sharp pain shot through my rib cage. I refused to believe my ears.

"You're late for what?" I shrugged my shoulders, pleading total ignorance.

"My period is late . . . and I . . ."

"And what? I always used condoms."

She appeared impatient. "Devin, nothing is one hundred percent."

"When are you going to get a test?"

"I took a test this morning . . ."

I tilted my head and mugged. "And . . ."

"Positive."

She was trying to ruin my life. "So, what now?"

"Devin, don't look at me like it's all my fault. We fucked up."

"We didn't do anything. I used a condom."

"Would you stop saying that stupid shit?"

"Stupid! Now this shit is stupid!" As I spit the words out of my mouth, I noticed we had become Starbucks' prime time special.

I walked out. "Perfect timing! Perfect fucking timing, Jennifer!"

She ran behind me. "Devin, I don't believe you're acting like this is all my fault. I don't believe you."

She cried harder. "Turn around and face me. Stop walking so fast. You're a coward."

Her words stung. Be a man, I repeated to myself. She had trapped me, and I couldn't run forever.

I turned around, both hands on my waist. "What do you want me to say? What do you want me to do?"

She walked in front of me, looked me up and down. "I want you to be a man."

"And how is that? Jump for joy?" If she was expecting that, she had the wrong man.

"At least ask me what I'm thinking. How I'm feeling? This is a shock for me, too. How do you think I feel carrying the baby of a man who's in love with another woman?" She sniffled. "I feel like shit. I feel like . . ." She cried harder. "I feel like it's not fair. I feel like I've been cheated."

She'd saved herself, only to give it away to a man whose heart belonged to someone else. From the moment she'd said she was late, I thought of Clark, never realizing that Jennifer was in pain, too.

I wrapped my arms around her. "You haven't been cheated, Jay. I'm going to do what I have to do. I'll support whatever decision you make." I prayed that she would make the right one.

She pulled away from me. "There is no decision. I'm having my baby."

Wanting to smack some sense into her, but the last thing I needed was a domestic violence charge, I replied, "Okay."

How did I get here? We quietly walked to her apartment. I went from blaming Clark to blaming Jennifer, back to blaming myself.

When there was really no one to blame. Shit happens. Seven hours prior, I had all the pieces to the confusing puzzle we call life.

Tears continued to roll down her round cheeks. I grabbed her hand to display some sign of condolence. As I attempted to intertwine my fingers in hers, I noticed my hand was shaking like a leaf. I wished everything would just disappear.

When we walked in her apartment, she rushed into her bedroom and came out with a Home Pregnancy Test, then handed it to me. "Here."

"So when exactly was your last period?"

"I guess about five weeks ago."

"What do you mean, you guess?"

"Look, Devin, you're going to have to change your attitude. This shit isn't going away."

What did she expect me to do? Act like after two months I was sure that I wanted her to have my baby.

"You know what, Jennifer, I need to go home. Take a nap. Think about what we're dealing with and I'll call you later."

I grabbed my coat from the arm of the sofa. Before I could get my balance, she yanked my arm, forcing me back to the couch to face her.

"So, you're going to just walk out?" The crying scene began again. "Devin, you know, I never thought you would act like this."

Jennifer acted like she was the only one in a predicament. Despite how cruel it appeared, I walked toward the door. Trying to console her with a gesture of sincerity, I said, "Jennifer, I'm not going anywhere. And trust me, I'm going to handle my responsibility. I just need time to digest this. I've taken in a whole lot in the last forty-eight hours."

She interjected, "What happened when you went to see Clark?"

"Jennifer, Clark has no business in this conversation. We have something else to deal with. I'm going home by myself, and I'll talk to you tomorrow."

As I walked out of the door, she whimpered like a sad pet hoping her owner would come rescue her. I couldn't. Devin needed to be saved first.

While I walked to my car, my entire life flashed before me. The visions frightened me.

Before I put the key in the ignition, I sat there. I watched the people walking the streets, hoping that a friend would appear.

Finally, I drove around the corner to my lonely home. My phone rang as I walked in. Clark. My heart plunged to my stomach. Frantically needing her support, her love, but determined not to answer. Standing still, I stared at the phone. Scared to move for fear that she was watching me. I slowly walked to my bedroom and lay across my bed. Sounds of anger and frustration escaped my body.

I jumped up, paced around. "This shit can't be happening. It can't be."

In desperate need of a friend, I picked up the phone to confess my sin to Clark. The phone rang twice. I came to my senses and hung up. Immediately after I pressed the flash button, my phone began to ring. My finger slipped. Damn. Slowly, I brought the phone back to my ear.

The voice on the other end broke the silence. "Devin, honey, what are you doing?" It was my mother. Whew.

"Hey, Mom. What's up?"

"I'm thinking about my little boy. How are your classes going?"

"Pretty good."

I wanted to share my problems with her, but I was scared that she would faint.

"So what else is going on?"

Maybe God sent her at that moment to heal my pain. "Mom, I am going through so much. You wouldn't believe it."

"Like what, Devin?"

I took a deep breath, decided that if Jennifer was having the baby, there was no better time than the present to let the truth be known.

"I got someone pregnant."

When the words came out, I felt like I'd made a mistake. I desperately wanted to eat the words. Was I that desperate for a friend? I paused, waiting for the lecture.

She spoke with a lump in her throat. "Devin, oh, no, I knew that she was going to do this."

Certain that she was speaking of Clark, I asked, "Who's she?"

"Clare."

She still refused to correctly speak Clark's name. I guess she hoped one day she wouldn't have to.

Embarrassed by my irresponsibility, I said, "It's not Clark."

I heard a sigh of relief. "Well, at least it's not that mean little witch."

I couldn't believe my ears. She despised Clark so much, she didn't care that I got someone pregnant, as long as it wasn't Clark. It disturbed me that she hated Clark, but I couldn't entertain it at the moment.

She continued, "Well, who is it, Devin?"

"You remember Jennifer, the one whose father is a judge in Michigan?" I had to provide her with Jennifer's family credentials.

"Oh, yeah." Surprisingly, she sounded like she approved. Maybe anyone is better than Clark.

"Yeah and she wants to have the baby."

"Devin, what are you going to do?"

"I guess I'm going to deal with it . . . I don't know."

Whenever my mother feels out of control, she walks back and forth in front of the window in her office. I could hear heels on the ceramic tile, which told me she was uncomfortable with my situation. She couldn't just swing her wand and make this one disappear.

"Devin, do you love this girl? How long have you been dating?"

Ashamed of the truth, I lied, "We've been dating since last year. It just became exclusive when I got back, two months ago."

"Oh, God! Devin, this is a mess."

Under my breath, I mumbled, "Tell me about it."

The problem solver sighed heavily as she thought of the next step.

"Devin, you didn't answer me. Do you love this girl?"

"Um, I don't know."

"Devin, you know how not to get someone pregnant. Please tell me that you love this girl."

"Yeah, I love her."

"Good."

Needing her to guide me, I asked, "Now what?"

"Has she told her family?"

I hadn't asked any meaningful questions. "I don't know."

"Devin." She spoke my name like she was disgusted. "You are going to be a man. You are going to bring Jennifer to meet us for Thanksgiving. We are going to work this whole thing out. If you love her, you will marry her before the baby is born. I refuse to have you fathering kids without committing to them."

Marriage is one thing that I was not going to be forced into. "No. I am not marrying her. I'm not in love with her like that."

"You loved her enough to get her pregnant."

Arguing wasn't going to help me. I conceded, "You're right."

"Devin, be responsible. Handle it with pride. I'll support you. I just don't want you to jeopardize your career."

"Mother, what do my career and this baby have in common?" It agitates me that my mother never sees people for who they really are inside. In her eyes, a person is a career.

She sighed. "Devin you have chosen a very affluent profession. Don't let anyone tell you that it doesn't matter how people perceive you. Having a child out of wedlock is a negative strike against you." She stressed, "Take it from me."

As I sat there, listening to her nonsense, I felt like shit. Can one mistake really affect the rest of my life? It scared me that I could possibly be facing the two most sacred things in life with the wrong person.

"I trust you." Honestly, at that moment, I believed in my mother. Pondering on her advice, I repeated, "I trust you."

"Devin, I love you. I'll call you later."

"Okay, I love you, too."

32

CLARK

How can a man reappear in your life, only to tear it apart? Why did he return my phone call? I didn't ask him to come here and tell me that we were going to make it. He left me to doctor two open wounds alone.

For the first time in years, I believed in him. I believed in us. I called and called, but no answer. I hoped he died, that way I could feel better about my stupidity. What kind of game was he playing? Three days passed, still no word. Why was my heart the target of his cruelty?

I couldn't sleep. Eating wasn't even a consideration. I ignored all of Troy's phone calls. I had no desire to see him. In less than four days, I lost five pounds. I needed to see him one last time before I could move on.

Before I realized the possible consequences of my actions, I was on Charles Street, buying a round-trip ticket to New York, carrying nothing but a purse. During the ride, my mind tried to reason with my heart, telling me to turn back. My heart demanded, "Keep on trucking." When I got to New York, it was about eleven o'clock at night. The city that never sleeps was still jumping, and so was my heart.

Lovesickness is a serious condition, and psychologists should take it more seriously. I looked like trash, but I had to see the man who was slowly and painfully murdering me. Finally, my turn came for a taxi.

Sanity tapped me on the shoulder as my brother's address came out of my mouth. "Ninety-seventh Street and Central Park West."

What was I supposed to tell Reggie? Feeling like a dummy around Reggie was nothing compared to the fool I'd be if I went to Devin's house. After all, what did I have to ask him? He'd made his point vividly clear. He didn't give a damn about me. He was a liar. This is the point where we say, "I should have left him when . . ."

One thing I've learned from this relationship is that honesty should never be sacrificed. I will never, as long as I live, make an excuse for a lying man. The truth may hurt initially, but it heals much better than the rigid scar caused by a lie. I dialed Reggie's number.

"Hey, Snook!" Sheena's happily in love voice greeted me.

"Hey, girl! Guess what?"

"What?"

"I'm about ten minutes from your house. Is it okay if I come over?" I asked, out of courtesy, but didn't expect she'd have the guts to tell me no.

"Sure. Come on. I need some company. Reggie's out of town for a few days."

"Okay. Good. I'm having an insane moment, and I could use a girls' night."

"I'll come down to the lobby and wait for you."

Before I got out of the taxi, Sheena was opening the door. "Hey, girl!"

I forced a smile. "Hey."

The closer I got into view, "Damn, Snook. You are a mess. What's going on?"

Before I spoke, she jumped in, "What the hell are you doing up here looking like you're searching for your lost dog?"

We both realized how true her statement could possibly be and started laughing. "I am."

When we got in the apartment, Sheena poured two glasses of

White Zinfandel. Before I could get my jacket off, I started telling the chain of events that had me in New York looking homeless.

She shook her head in disbelief. "Snook. Do you think something happened to him?"

"I keep trying to find answers, but that inner me is saying that his sorry ass is fine."

She laughed because she knew I was right. I talked and we drank. Every reference I made to sorry men, she would cosign. I sensed that things weren't so perfect on the home front.

After four glasses or so, Sheena loosened up. "Clark, girl. Dudes are no damn good, including your brother."

Dying to know why she felt that way, I edged her on. "Why do you say that?"

"'Cause every time he goes out of town, he flies out of Baltimore." She gave me an inquisitive look. "What the hell is that all about?"

I pleaded the fifth. I hope she didn't think I was going to snitch. "I don't know, Sheena." I shrugged my shoulders. "Maybe he likes to see the kids. That's what I've always thought."

"Yeah. Me, too."

"So, what are you saying?"

"I'm saying, you don't have to confirm or deny, but I think he's creeping with Tanisha."

I had issues of my own, and I definitely didn't come prepared to tackle the monster that she had let loose.

I attempted to erase any thought of the possibility. "Girl, you know Tanisha is my girl." I tried to sound convincing. I put emphasis on every syllable. "I would know. She is madly in love with Fred." I tried to stress it. "Trust me."

I did the same thing that I resented in Devin. I lied, but my reason was worthy. Right?

"If you say so." She twisted her neck. "But, if I ever catch him cheating, the wedding is off." She held her right hand up like she was swearing. "And I mean it, Clark. I refuse to put up with a cheating man. I won't."

Veins bulged from her temples like she was having visions of infidelity. Her eyes looked like she knew something, but just couldn't put her finger on it. I had nothing to tell her. I had no evidence that he was sleeping with Tanisha. Nor was I willing to accept that everyone I really love was betraying me. I tried to console Sheena in the midst of my own pain. "Girl, I know how you feel, but I honestly think my brother is tired of running."

If nothing more than my personal reassurance, I hoped my statement was true. I desperately needed to believe that there were still some honest men left in the world.

She shook her head, obviously wanting to disclose more evidence, but she refrained. "I hope so, Clark. I really do."

Strategically, I reverted back to my own dilemma. We talked for another hour or so, constantly drinking. Then, out of the blue, she burst out. "You didn't come all the way up here to talk about it. Let's go over there. Hell, you deserve some answers!"

Sheena got up, started looking for her keys. It was like she was going to war for every female with a broken heart. She stormed through the house, grabbed her purse, and slipped on her shoes. I sat still.

She yanked me. Her speech slurred. "Let's go! It is time to go. You don't have to take this shit. If more of us went off on their asses, maybe they wouldn't try this dumb shit."

Despite my intoxication, I wasn't equipped for rejection. I needed to have a civilized conversation to determine why he lied. Certainly, I couldn't get that on a surprise visit in the middle of the night.

"No, Sheena, I'm not going."

She pulled me. "You have to go. You have to."

She appeared more concerned about my battle than me. "Why? Why is it so important to you that I go?"

"Because you gotta face it. You have to. That's the only way. If you don't face it, you'll live in denial forever." She disguised her drunkenness and tried to sound reasonable. "You ever heard someone died? You knew it was true, but you really couldn't accept it 'til you saw the body?"

I nodded. With that, I stood to my feet. "Let's go. You're right. I came up here to face it. And damn it, I'm gonna face it."

I grabbed my coat and forced myself to prepare for the worst.

Two drunk, scorned women, we hiked uptown. When we got close to Devin's building, I got scared. Hesitation was indubitably written on my face. She looked at me and grasped my hand. "Don't get scared now, girl. I'm your sister and I got you."

There is power in numbers, because I would have never had the courage without Sheena. We walked up the steps to Devin's apartment. Nervous giggles after every step or so. I kept saying, "I don't believe you got me out here acting like a fool."

When we got to the door, I gave Sheena a look of uncertainty. She knocked before I could turn around. Finally, I heard footsteps. I knew the bastard was alive. Up to the very moment, I wouldn't erase the possibility that someone had robbed and beaten him to death. I searched for an explanation for his blatant disrespect.

"Who is it?"

I yelled, "Clark."

He whispered, "What the fuck?"

Sheena answered, "Yeah, we got the same question, Mothafucker!"

I looked at her. "Let me handle this!"

She smiled. "I'm going to sit in the lobby. If you need me, hit me on the cell."

She took off down the hall just as Devin opened the door. He was a horrific sight. His hair was matted like he'd been asleep for days. His eyes were fire red. I wanted to zap out—scream, yell, bite, and kick—instead I just looked at him.

He didn't open the door wide enough to welcome me. So I asked what I came to ask, "Why, Devin? Why did you come back into my life and make me feel like we had a chance?"

He shrugged his shoulders. He didn't say a word. Say something! I gave him four of the best years of my life. I loved him with every beat of my heart. I killed my baby for him, and he couldn't say anything.

Anger empowered me. I kicked the door, trying to make him open it. He wouldn't let go. I stuck my foot in the door and began shoving with my shoulder. Finally, he gave up. I started throwing punches at him. Inside his pitch-black apartment, I wailed, "Why?"

Swinging in continuous motion, I repeated, "Why?"

He cried, "I'm sorry, Clark."

Trying to purge the evil trapped inside, I beat at his chest. In between my whooping, he sobbed. He pleaded, "I'm sorry. I didn't mean to hurt you."

I tripped over something on the floor and fell to my knees. I began to weep. Useless energy exerted, because I still felt like shit. He bent down to hold me, and immediately someone flicked the light switch. I looked up and saw a ghost. Jennifer stood fully dressed, built like a gladiator. She lacked femininity. Her hair hung wildly like a flower child's. It baffled me how he could choose her over me. He denied me for a muscle woman. Wanting to lunge at her, but realizing it wasn't her fault, I gave Devin an inquisitive stare.

Embarrassed that she witnessed my breakdown, I jumped up and regained my composure. I ran for the door. When I reached the door, Devin was behind me. I turned and looked deep in his eyes.

Before I could spit in his face, the same tune again, "Clark, I'm sorry."

He reached out to touch my hand. I pulled back and dashed out into the hallway. The look, the way he reached out for me, he wanted to tell me something. I came to get peace, but I left with more questions.

I walked down into the lobby, feeling barren. Devin needed me. In the four years I'd known him, never had I seen him so vulnerable. His eyes disturbed me.

When I reached the lobby, Sheena was slumped down in a hard plastic chair. I tried to wake her, but she didn't budge. Luckily, I didn't need her for backup. Jennifer dashed out of the front door without acknowledging us. I decided to go back and try the calm approach.

I scurried back up to Devin's apartment, in a more settled state. He opened the door like he was awaiting my return. I stepped in, and he turned on the light. I walked over to the couch and sat down. Devin walked over slowly and sat on the opposite end. I began, "Devin, I just wanted some answers. Don't you think I deserve that?"

He nodded.

"I don't think I'm being unreasonable."

His eyes watered, and he sniffled. "Clark, I wasn't trying to hurt you. Everything I said when I saw you, I meant it." He shook his head. "I just . . ."

"What?" I pleaded. "Why couldn't you just call me and say you changed your mind?"

"Because I didn't change my mind. I . . ." he stuttered.

"What the hell do you mean? You didn't change your mind. You're laid up here with Diamond the Gladiator." He snickered a little, knowing my facetious reference was accurate. "You haven't answered any of my calls. I left desperate messages on your machine. I just wanted to know if you were dead or alive." I paused. "You couldn't give me that."

"You wouldn't understand what I'm going through."

"You know what. You're probably right. There should be nothing that you're going through that you shouldn't be able to tell me. If it's that bad you chose to treat me like shit, instead of being a man and confronting me, maybe I can't understand."

I slid to the edge of the sofa and put my hand on my hip. I looked at him as if to say, "Now tell me what the hell is wrong with you."

He hung his head in shame. "Jennifer's pregnant."

"She's what?"

"Pregnant. And I just don't know my head from my ass right now." He let out a heavy sigh, like a weight was lifted from his chest.

"So, you want to treat me like shit, because you're irresponsible. You're right. I don't understand. That still doesn't explain why you haven't returned my damn calls."

"I know, Clark. That was fucked up, but I've been in the house all week. My head is throbbing. I haven't talked to anyone. I'm just fucked up right now."

"You know what? I'm fucked up, too. How could you be sleeping with two women without protection? I thought you were smarter than that."

He didn't argue. "I thought I was smart, too."

I hoped he'd at least say the condom broke, but nothing. I wished so bad that there was a possibility that it wasn't his baby. From his expression, I could tell that he was convinced. "So, what is she going to do?"

"She's having it."

I wanted to curl up and die. "What do you want?"

"I mean, I didn't want a baby right now. And more than that, I don't want a baby by her, but I can't convince her to do something that she doesn't want to do to her body."

My mind rapidly shifted back to when I did exactly that. I besmirched my body for Devin's love. Too afraid to burden him with the responsibility, I sacrificed my baby's life for his future. I envied Jennifer. She was able to separate the love of self from the love of a man. I'd disrupted my peace so Devin could have life more abundantly. How can love be so blind?

I snapped out of my daydream after I heard Devin call my name several times.

"What?"

"Clark, can you just hold me?"

I wrapped my arms around him, because I needed affection as well.

"Thank you, baby. Thank you so much. I needed you. I'm glad you came."

I vowed to myself that I would never say a word about my experience. At that moment, I felt like he needed to know, but I suppressed the desire. Once again, I forfeited my feelings for Devin's sake.

"I still really don't understand why you thought you couldn't talk to me."

"I was scared that you would never want to speak to me again. I thought you would feel like it should be you having my baby, if anyone."

He added gas to the flame that was already burning. I shook my head. "I do feel that way."

"And I felt like it would be best for me to just disappear and you would never have to deal with it."

Baffled by his ignorant solution, "You thought I would just let you disappear?"

He forced a chuckle. "Man, I've been going through it this week. I don't know. I really wasn't thinking.

"When you came here, I wanted to run and hide in a closet. I didn't want to face you. Shit, I don't know."

"Devin, you know what, I am really mad right now, but I hope you never feel like you can't talk to me. If it's over and you want to be with Jennifer and the baby, I'll deal with it. It's going to be hard as hell, but I will get over you."

"Clark, don't leave me like this."

"What are you saying? What do you want from me, Devin?"

"Honestly, I don't know, but I'm not ready to let you go. That's why I didn't want to talk to you until I sorted everything out."

"You're crazy."

"No, I'm not. Just tell me that you got my back. I promise I'll make a decision soon."

Why did I feel sorry for him after all the heartache he'd caused me? I stood up and opened my arms. After all, I did love the man. The thought of it being our last embrace intimidated me, so I let go. "Okay, Devin, I have to go."

"You're not going to stay."

"No, I think it would be best if I go. I don't want to stay with you until you've made up your mind."

He hugged me again. "I understand."

I rushed for the door before I got trapped in his captivity. Before I walked out, I turned and pecked him on the lips, keeping it superficial. He pulled me to him and kissed me slowly. Then he looked directly in my eyes. Sincerity lurked in his pupils. "Clark, I love you. You know that, right?"

Afraid to return his condolence, I just shook my head and casually waved. I mouthed gently, "Bye, bye."

33

DEVIN

From my bedroom window, I stared at the sky. For the first time all week, I took responsibility for my leading role in the play of events. Two women had walked through my door in tears. My baby grows inside one, and my heart desperately cries out for the other. How could I choose?

My phone rang. I prayed Clark had decided to come back.

"Hello."

"Devin."

"What's up, Jay?"

"Can I come back? I wasn't finished."

"Sure."

Shortly after I hung up, she tapped on the door. When I opened the door, she gently rubbed my face.

"Devin, you have to snap out of it. It's not the end of the world."

That was the simple solution to it all. Despite all the stress I was causing myself, life goes on. Either I'd lose Clark or I'd have a child out of wedlock. It was quite that simple.

Jennifer poured water into the kettle. "Devin, do you want some tea?"

"Yeah."

I sat on the couch and turned the television on. It was going on a total of five days without sleep. She walked from the kitchen with two mugs.

"Here, Devin."

She sat beside me. "Like I told you earlier, I just want the best for the baby. I want to be with you. I want a family, but if you don't, we'll make it. Okay?"

I nodded. Despite my silence, I absorbed every word.

After another hour of pleading her case, she made one last request. "Devin, if we aren't going to be together, please stay close enough to us, so you can be a part of our child's life. Okay?"

Partially lethargic, I agreed. No longer viewing her as the enemy, we fell asleep on the living room floor. When the sun rose, I rubbed my eyes. Beside me, she lay. Full of uncertainty, she slept peacefully. Life growing inside of her, she glowed in the midst of the pain. How could I be so cruel?

34

CLARK

Armed with an excuse for why he'd hurt me, I slept like a baby on the train ride home. When I got off the train, I realized that I was supposed to go with Tanisha to try on wedding gowns. I rushed home and changed my clothes.

When I walked into Tanisha's house, Fred was standing in the living room like he was about to leave.

"Hey, Fred."

"What's up, Clark?"

"Nothing much."

"Why you been dissing my boy? He said he hasn't talked to you all week."

I didn't comment.

"You know that shit ain't right."

Devin had hurt me. As a result, I was hurting Troy.

When Tanisha walked down the stairs, she walked up to him and kissed him. "Baby, we're about to go."

He looked at her like Devin used to look at me. I turned my head to stare at the empty wall, trying to conceal the jealousy.

He laughed. "Clark, make sure you hook my baby up."

"I will."

Tanisha smiled at him. "Are you trying to say I need help? You don't think I have a sense of style?"

From behind, he put his hands on her shoulders and began to

massage. The last place I needed to be was in the midst of lovers. Though I was happy for Tanisha, unconsciously her happiness told me that I was not worthy.

I walked to the front door, before I was forced to watch another gesture of endearment. Immediately, Tanisha walked out behind me. Fred came next. He said, "Damn, Clark. Why you run out like that?"

"We need to hurry, because the bridal shops get crowded."

Fred waved his hand. "Yeah, whatever."

He kissed his bride-to-be one last time, making every moment memorable.

Before she could get in the car good, she growled, "What the hell is your problem this morning?"

"I was just ready to go."

"No." She accused, "You have an attitude, and I want to know why."

I snapped, "Look, I am just trying to get to the stores before they get crowded."

Why did I think I could fool Tanisha? "Clark Anderson. I know something is wrong with you, but the point is, I need you to be supportive today. If you are not in the mood, then tell me. I can find someone else to go."

How could I tell her about the weekend, about Jennifer's pregnancy? She'd made it painfully clear that I was not the center of attention.

I gave a bullshit excuse for my attitude. "Nish, I'm just a little down, and maybe I have been acting nasty this morning. I'm sorry."

She didn't look at me. She just nodded and said, "Yeah, I know how it is, but I hope you can suppress your little attitude."

When we walked into the bridal shop, it was just in time for her appointment. The sales associate took some of the weight off of my back. She did all of the talking. Finally, we all agreed on a few dresses for her to try on. They all were typically the same, a tightly fitted sleeveless top, with the princess tulle bottom. We agreed that the style complemented Tanisha's pear-shaped body. The lady went into the dressing room to help. I stood there, looking around at all the girls trying on their gowns. I despised that they all had been granted a stamp of approval from a man who apparently loved them. I tried staring at the ceiling, but mirrors were everywhere. White gowns, veils, and trains blocked every possible mental outlet. Just as I was about to flee, Tanisha walked out of the dressing room. The commotion stopped. Other people looked at her in admiration. She didn't have on a lick of makeup, and still she made the whole room pause. For the first time all day, I felt excited. At least one of us had someone who cared enough to ask.

She bashfully stepped up to the pedestal, as she was totally aware that all eyes were on her. I said, "Girl, you are the bomb. You look so good."

She smiled. "Thank you. Do you really like it?"

"Yeah. This is the one."

She nodded. "I think so."

She didn't try on another gown. Once she put her clothes on, my attitude had lightened up. When we got out of the shop, Tanisha put her arm around my shoulders. "Clark, don't sit around and wait for him. Don't let him hold the key to your happiness. You have to be the one to decide what's going to be."

I looked at her as if to say, "How can you say that when Reggie had you on a leash for years?"

Noticing the question mark on my face, she clarified, "I know from experience. And look." She opened her arms like she had come up short. "He didn't choose me. I wish I would have left him a long time ago. Sometimes we stay in stuff because we're scared to let go. When in reality, all we need to do is let go. Girl, if it's meant to be, it will be."

Who was the clown that first said, "If it's meant to be, it will be"? Surely, it doesn't heal a broken heart. It only causes the brain to go berserk wondering if it will be.

I tried to accept the message and not judge the messenger. After she gave her motivational speech, I told her about Jennifer. "Clark, I'm so sorry. Why didn't you say something? I would have changed my appointment if I'd known all that went on this weekend."

35

DEVIN

In order to get my thoughts straight, I restricted communication with Clark to one to two times a week. She deserved to be the champion in the end, but I'm uncomfortable with having my baby grow up in a home without me. I spent more and more time with Jennifer, forcing my feelings to grow.

Intoxication and the thought of those shorts in Clark's room helped me to restrain my true longing. My mother's daily phone calls were also weapons against poor Clark.

Jennifer stopped pressuring me. Her family supported her decision financially and emotionally, whether we married or not. She had regressed to being the peaceful young lady that won my heart. Watching her stomach grow made me gravitate to her.

Jennifer sat on my bed, watching me dress to go out. For the first time, in almost four weeks, I actually put on something other than sweats. I felt clean with my black slacks and a gray turtleneck on. I didn't plan to think about Clark or Jennifer while in the club.

"You look good, Devin."

Playfully, I pulled her from the bed and danced around. She laughed. "Alright, boy, I'm going home."

As she walked to the door, I followed. "Go home and get some rest."

Her face beamed. "Alright. Call me when you get in."

"Okay."

Moments after she left, I was in my car pumping, "The Players Anthem." I vowed to scope out everything with two legs, just because I could.

After standing in line for almost a half hour, I was finally in the club. The bar was my first stop. After a few sips of Hennessy, I felt it. After maneuvering on the dance floor for twenty minutes, sweat poured off of me like a waterfall. I was there, alone, dancing like I brought the party with me.

One girl eyed me from the time I stepped on the floor. Initially, I thought we inadvertently made contact. After four times, she was obviously attracted. She was about Clark's size, with a deep brown complexion. Her hair was cut short, but sexy as hell. She wore tight leather pants and a strapless top. I danced over to her and asked if she wanted to dance. She happily joined me.

After we both sweated our high away, I asked, "Would you like another drink?"

"Sure."

"I'll be right back."

I turned to walk to the bar. She grabbed my hand and suggested we go downstairs instead. The basement of Club Cheetah is where everyone mingles.

We headed down the steps. It took us a few moments to make it through the crowd. Because my high was coming down, the stop-and-go frustrated me.

When we got to the bottom of the steps, the first person I saw standing at the bar was Reggie. Not in the mood for small talk, I suggested we go back upstairs.

She insisted, "No, it's too crowded. I want to stay down here and chill for a while."

Reluctantly, I conceded, "Okay."

Once Reggie grabbed his drink, he turned around. Eye to eye. He gritted on me, as usual. I returned the arrogant mug.

He dropped the two drinks on the floor. Without one spoken word, he hit me in the jaw. He stunned me. I tried to brace myself, but he was all over me like a tiger. We started rumbling. I heard gasps from the crowd as we rolled around on the floor. Finally, the bouncers came to carry us out. Everything happened so fast. I had absolutely no idea why the fight took place.

While the bouncers were separating us, he snarled, "Nigga, that's for my sister! You punk-bitch! Don't ever disrespect her again!"

You would have thought I cheated on him the way he acted. Damn. While I was being dragged out, I knew that Clark was no longer the one for me. Jennifer was my final decision. God had to bang me in the mouth for me to hear His voice.

When I got outside of the club, the line was still long. Blood dripped from my lip. My jaw throbbed. Praying no one would recognize me, I zipped past the line, looking in the opposite direction.

I jogged toward the car. When I got in my car, I sat there for a moment to catch my breath. Then I dialed Clark's number.

She answered like she was asleep. "What's up?"

"Why the fuck would you tell your brother about Jennifer?"

She woke up instantaneously. "Devin, what are you talking about?"

I could have gotten arrested. That one stupid incident could have ruined my career. I yelled, "Your dumb-ass brother just jumped me in the club."

"Did y'all get into an argument or something?"

Her ignorance made me angry. "No. The fool just ran up and hit me. I didn't say a damn thing to him. He said it was for you."

"I don't believe my brother would just run up on you and hit you."

I imagined her doubtful expression and got pissed. "Fuck it! You don't have to believe me."

She mumbled, "Oh, shit!"

Curious as to what she was thinking, I asked, "Oh, shit, what?"

She took a breath. "Devin, I'm sorry."

"What?" I snapped. "You told him to jump me?"

"No. I would never do that."

She was too damn calm. Her tone irritated me. "Then, tell me what you're talking about."

She sighed. "When I came back from Phoenix, I told Reggie what happened. You know, how you raped me."

Annoyed by her accusation, I growled, "You say I raped you. I didn't rape you and you know it."

"Devin, you did."

"You say I did. I don't remember. For all I know, you could have made it all up."

She yelled, "You did! I'm not crazy. I know what you did to me!"

She caught herself in the middle of her excitement. She stopped abruptly, afraid to upset me more. She sniffed. "Devin, I'm sorry about Reggie. He was just angry. I don't know what got into him."

"Man, you know what, fuck this bullshit. I'm out!"

I hung up the phone. There was no doubt in my mind that I loved Clark and she loved me, too, but it was best for us to be apart. Everything happens for a reason. She could believe that my decision was based on the altercation with Reggie. I wouldn't have to deal with the burden of her broken heart on my shoulders. She could share the blame.

She called back repeatedly. I wanted to answer my phone, but breaking away while I was angry was best. I would never have enough balls to hurt Clark in any other state of mind. I turned my phone off and turned my back on the past.

When I walked in my apartment, I went straight to the bathroom to look at my face. My lip had a lump the size of a nickel. My jaw sat out like a golf ball was stuck there. The skin under my eye was red. I couldn't spend another night alone with the reflection staring at me. I walked in the room and called Jennifer.

She answered, "Hello."

"Hey, Jay." I tried to sound cheerful.

"Did you have fun tonight?"

"No, I got in a beef with some crazy dude at the bar." I didn't want her to think that the fight with Reggie was what forced me to make my decision. If I was going to be with her, I didn't want her to feel like a second-hand woman.

She giggled, obviously thinking that I was crazy.

"Devin, how did you get in a fight? What happened?"

I made up some silly story about wasting a drink on some guy's suede shoes. She just listened and didn't doubt a word. All she cared about was that I was okay. She was at my door in a matter of seconds.

All through the night, I held her. She and the life inside of her belonged to me. My lady, she loved me, and I would grow to love her.

36

CLARK

After I heard Devin's answering machine for the fiftieth time, I called Reggie on his cell phone. He picked up. Loud music blasted in my ear.

"Reggie!"

"Snook, I fucked that clown up." I could tell by his voice that he had surpassed the legal limit.

"I know. Now he won't talk to me."

"Why you dealing with a clown that raped you? See, girls are stupid."

He didn't understand. "Reggie, that's not the point. I wanna know why you're walking around fighting like you're fifteen years old."

He tried to explain his irrational behavior. "I didn't expect you to react like that." He laughed an alcoholic chuckle. "When I saw his face, I thought about him abusing my baby. Man, I just snapped. I don't know what got into me."

Maybe I was the stupid one for dealing with him after the episode, but I loved him. Isn't that enough reason to forgive someone?

He fought Devin because he loves me. How could I be mad?

"Well, I want you to go home. You sound like you've been drinking too much."

"I'm on my way. Sheena just called. You know she'll have a fit if I don't get there soon."

I snickered. Sheena had the player in check. "Okay, Reggie. Call me tomorrow."

"I love you." Instead of appreciating the sincere affection from my brother, I wished it were Devin telling me those three significant words.

"I love you, too."

I hung up and cried myself to sleep.

37

DEVIN

Jennifer and I sat on the plane, headed to Phoenix for Thanksgiving. She slept and I watched. I looked at her and thought about the ring in my pocket. Could I really make her my wife? I nervously tapped on my knee. I questioned my love, but felt obligated to my child.

When the limo stopped in front of my parents' house, they were standing in the doorway. When Jennifer stepped out, Leona anxiously rushed over to the car.

"Hello, honey."

She hugged Jennifer and stepped back. She stretched Jennifer's arms open. "I can't believe I'm going to be a grandmother."

Jennifer chuckled. "I can't believe it either."

I was forcing myself to accept it more and more with each passing day.

My dad helped me roll the luggage into the house. When we finally got settled, my mom gave Jennifer the tour. I sat in the kitchen and had the father-son talk that we hadn't had since I was eighteen. He plunged into the conversation.

"Devin, well, at least she's beautiful."

We laughed. "That's always a plus."

"And I guess she's smart."

I laughed. "Yeah, she is that."

"Look, Devin, I know this may sound unreasonable to you now, but as you get older, you'll understand it more and more. Sometimes you don't marry for love. Sometimes it just makes sense."

Though I had already concluded that, I asked, "What do you mean?"

"Your mother and I got married when we were in law school, because we were broke. We needed each other financially. Now we never have to worry about money again, and we love each other. Love is just an emotion that grows for whoever you chose."

"Is it really that simple?"

He nodded. "It was for me."

Within seconds, the cackling hens walked in. My mom smiled from ear to ear. "Devin, Jennifer's going to stay in the pool house with you."

Baffled. I spat out, "What?"

She patted Jennifer's belly. "Well, Devin, you guys have done about all there is to be done now."

We all found that funny. Jennifer said, "I'm going to go and get ready for bed. I'm really tired."

Left alone with my parents, I was suddenly grilled by both of them. My mother said, "Son, she's special. You're not going to meet a lot of women like her."

My dad added, "You two have a lot in common, and you're about to have a child."

My eyes shifted from one to the other. When I finally got tired of the lecture, I pulled the ring from my back pocket. They gasped.

My mother said, "I knew I reared a good man and that you'd eventually accept your responsibility. I'm so proud of you."

My father nodded. "I think you're doing the right thing."

My mother asked, "When are you going to ask?"

"Whenever the time is right."

My mother hugged me. "That's all I can ask you to do. If you need anything, you know we're here."

"I know."

When I walked into the pool house, Jennifer was already in the bed. I stood at the bedside. "You need anything, Jay?"

"Some ginger ale or something. I feel sick."

I rushed into the house to get her something to drink. When I got back, she was sitting up in the bed, holding her head. "Devin, I have a headache."

I rubbed her back and held the glass to her mouth. She looked at me and mumbled, "I'm so lucky to have you."

"I'm lucky to have you, too."

She stretched out sideways and drifted off to sleep. I took my clothes off and slipped in behind her. I held her in the spoon position and rubbed her stomach.

I was awakened by Jennifer's discomfort. She tossed and turned. I looked at the clock. Four o'clock in the morning. I felt like I'd been asleep for only twenty minutes. Suddenly, a feeling surrounded me.

I tapped her shoulder. She groaned. "Yeah, baby?"

"Jennifer."

Her eyes were still closed. I walked over to flick the light on. I whispered, "Jay."

She peeled her eyes open. "What's up, Devin?"

I grabbed the ring from my pants and kneeled beside the bed. She stared at me like I was insane. "Jennifer, you know there was a time when I didn't know what I wanted. When I didn't know what I was feeling. But I'm falling deeper and deeper in love with you."

Hoping that she wasn't dreaming, she sat up and touched my arm. I continued, "Each time I think about the baby, our baby that grows inside of you, I get chills. It used to scare me, because I didn't know what I wanted, but now I'm sure."

Her eyes widened.

"Jennifer, will you marry me?"

She sat on the side of the bed and began to kiss me. "Yes, Devin. Yes. I'll marry you."

38

CLARK

Troy took me to a Christmas celebration on the *Odyssey* cruise in D.C. He was in my life, but my heart belonged to Devin. Troy was slowly becoming more of a friend than a prospect. I was afraid to have sex with him, because I knew of all his other relationships. I was afraid to give him too much time for fear of falling in love again.

We slow danced the entire night. We kissed, and for the first time, I began to feel something different. He felt it, too, because he bent down and kissed me again. I held him tightly. Could I actually share my love with him?

I rubbed his back and laid my head on his chest. I wished he were Devin, but he wasn't. If you can't be with the one you love, love the one you're with.

When the boat docked, people casually exited. Troy and I stood in the middle of the floor. I stared into his eyes, hoping to find that special something. The romantic moment was interrupted by a familiar voice. "Clark?"

My heart sank. I turned to see Devin's closest friend, Jason. I felt ashamed that I was bumping and grinding with a new man so soon, until I looked into his eyes. He touched my shoulder, sympathy in his expression. "Damn, Clark."

I smiled tightly, afraid to expose my vulnerability. I hugged him, trying to lift the burden. "Jason, what's going on?"

"Nothing, Clark. I'm glad to see you're doing well."

I turned to introduce Troy. He was gone. Jason chuckled. "It looks like your date left."

I smiled. "He's around somewhere."

"So, who you here with?"

"This chick that works with me. I guess she's around somewhere, too."

I nodded. "That's good."

Then an intense moment of silence invaded our space. He needed to say something. I wanted to ask about Devin. We both sighed. I hugged him again. "Alright, man. Good seeing you. Go find your date."

He took one last look at me. He mumbled, "Hey, Clark."

My eyes widened. "What's up, Jason?"

He took a deep breath. "Take care."

He shook my hand and slowly pulled away. Seeing him connected me with Devin. In seconds, he was gone.

As I stood there reminiscing, Troy's voice startled me. "C'mon. You ready?"

He appeared agitated. I grabbed his hand, silently apologizing for ignoring his presence. When we finally got to my car, an envelope was on my front window. The outside said, *But he still loves you*, written like the person was in a rush. I pulled the card out of the envelope. Stunned, I stared at the card. I leaned against the door. My knees buckled.

Troy walked around to my side. "What's wrong?"

I struggled for air. I fell into my car. Hoping to change the words I saw. Nothing changed. My heart felt like it was being ripped from my chest and chopped into tiny pieces. I read it again:

Because you are a special friend,
We would like to invite you to share our love as we become one
Thursday, the Thirty-first Day of December,
Nineteen Hundred and Ninety-Eight at Six O'clock P.M.
At the Waldorf Astoria Hotel, 301 Park Avenue
New York, New York 10022

Devin Patterson & Jennifer Shaw

Troy gazed at the invitation with me. He began to shake his head. He walked around to the passenger side. He said, "Can you open the door?"

Why did Jason feel he needed to give me the message? If Devin still loved me, why was he marrying Jennifer? Questions raced through my head like field mice. I unlocked the doors. I needed to scream, but I couldn't. I wanted to cry, but I couldn't. I fumbled to put the key in the ignition.

In an irritated tone, Troy asked, "Do you want me to drive while you get yourself together?"

"No, I'm fine."

How could he have the audacity to marry her so soon?

Troy didn't speak the entire ride back to my apartment. Finally, when we got out of the car, he spoke.

"Clark, we've been going out for four months or so, and I've watched you go through this bullshit. You love ol' boy. Even though, I think you deserve better."

He shook his head. "You deserve so much more. But you won't get over that dude until you fight for him. If you love him that much, fight for him."

"Fight for him? He's about to get married."

He pulled me to him. "He's not married yet. The thing that I like most about you is that you're strong. You go for what you want. This ain't no different."

His eyes glistened. He put one hand on my shoulder. As if it was too painful to utter, he took a deep breath and shook his head. "I can't sit around and watch you chase him." He pounded his fist into mine. "I'm out." With his infamous farewell, he strolled to his car. Dumbfounded, I watched my friend roll out of my life.

I dashed into the apartment and rushed to the phone. There had to be a viable explanation. I dialed Devin's cell phone. Disconnected. I dialed his home phone. Number changed to an unlisted number.

Days went by; still the invitation sat on my nightstand. Wanting so badly for him to call and say it was a prank, I waited by the phone. With each setting of the sun, I accepted more and more that the invitation was real. Devin was about to be another woman's husband. He was about to make the decision of his life and hadn't even given me an opportunity for closure.

I picked up the phone. The receptionist on the other end cheerfully answered, "Waldorf Astoria Hotel."

I paused. "I would like to make reservations for"—I debated—"the Patterson wedding on December thirty-first."

39

DEVIN

Just moments before my wedding ceremony, my boy Jason and I stood in the hall waiting for the time to go in. My confidence was decreasing with each passing second.

When the time finally arrived, I followed Jason. I heard Clark's raspy voice call me. Initially, I thought I was dreaming. Then I turned to see her little head peeking from the stairwell. Uncertain of what I should do, I paused.

I yelled to Jason, "Hold up, man. I'm coming."

I ducked into the stairwell. She stood there wearing a beautiful, white strapless dress. She looked like a bride. I rubbed my eyes. Could it be my imagination?

She reached out and touched me. Her hand sent chills up my spine. I yanked back.

She pleaded, "Devin, I . . . I . . ."

My heart wanted to reach out and embrace her, but my mind cautioned me. I couldn't move. I was paralyzed by her presence.

She continued, "I know that you still love me."

I shook my head. I begged her, "Clark, don't do this. Not on my wedding day."

She walked closer to me. Our bodies practically touched. Her warmth reminded me of the good times. She looked at me. Her eyes told the story of our love.

Softly, she spoke. "Devin, I have loved you my entire adult life.

I can't watch you walk down the aisle with a woman that I know you don't love."

Her scent hypnotized me. I wanted to throw it all away. My conscience scolded me. I staggered backward, shaking my head constantly. I clenched my teeth together. "Clark, I don't love you anymore."

She pulled my arm. I tried to pry away. She gripped with both hands. Her eyes flooded. "Devin, you're making a big mistake."

I took a deep, agitated breath. "Clark, I love Jennifer."

As the words escaped my mouth, Clark cracked. Tears began to roll. "Devin, I don't believe you. You don't believe you."

I demanded, "Clark, look! You heard what I said. I love her."

She looked deep into my eyes. "Do you? Do you really love her?"

I nodded. She shook her head. "If you love her, there's nothing left for me to say."

She began to walk up the stairs. In between sniffles, she said, "I was never good enough for you anyway."

I wanted to run behind her, but I couldn't. How could I disappoint my family, Jennifer's family? I pulled the door and mumbled, "I love you, Clark."

I jogged down the hall to catch Jason. He stood there baffled. "Where'd you go, man?"

"Man, I went in the stairwell to pray."

He shook my hand. "I don't blame you, dawg."

We rushed in the ballroom through a side door. Immediately, the procession began. I looked out at all the people. My eyes shifted from the back door to the side door. Did Clark complete her mission or did she have something else planned? My stomach rumbled. My eyes blurred. My body swayed back and forth. Jason tapped me. "Yo, you cool?"

I nodded. All the guests stood. The pianist began to play, "Here Comes the Bride."

Clark appeared in the doorway. What the fuck? All the guests gasped. She killed Jennifer. She tied her up. As my mind continued to play tricks on me, Jennifer slowly walked down the aisle. My nerves did somersaults. My jaw dropped. She was more stunning than ever. My eyes watered. Visions of Clark slowly faded. My wife-to-be stood before me. Her innocent smile greeted me.

After a short prayer and a scripture, the minister said, "Who gives this woman to be married to this man?"

Her father said, "I do."

He stepped away. She held my sticky hand and looked at me inquisitively. I attempted to conceal my thoughts. She offered me this ever so forgiving look of understanding. My heart sank.

As I said my vows, my eyes shifted from her belly to her eyes. For my child, I will sacrifice myself, my needs, and my desires. "To you, I thee wed."

The minister announced, "I now pronounce you husband and wife. You may kiss the bride."

I bent down to lift her veil. Clark's smile startled me. I yanked my head back. The guests laughed, as did Jennifer. If only they knew the thoughts lurking in my head. When I kissed her, I closed my eyes tightly to block out Clark's face. Our bond was made with Clark's spirit in the midst.

40

CLARK

I sat in the hotel room alone and drank an entire bottle of Hennessy. I stretched out on the bed and missed the coming of the New Year. When I woke up, it was ten o'clock. I looked at my cell phone. Fifteen missed calls. Who the hell?

My phone started to ring just as I was about to check my messages.

"Hello."

My mother cried hysterically on the other end. "Clark, where are you?"

"I'm in New York. Why? What's wrong?"

"It's Tanisha. Just hurry up and get here!"

"What's wrong?"

"I just want you to hurry up. We need you here. I've been calling you all day. Hurry up, baby."

I began shaking. "Mama, please tell me something. Where is Reggie? Is he in New York?"

"No, baby, Reggie is here. Just hurry up! We will meet you at Tanisha's grandmother's house. We're all here."

I made a mad dash for my car. How was I supposed to get back to Baltimore in one piece? Why is God giving me an overdose of drama? Scared to let my mind wonder about what was going on with Tanisha, I tried to sing the songs on the radio.

It took me forever to get out of the city. There was bumper-to-bumper traffic. Why was I being intentionally tortured? After I finally got out of the congested city, I drove 120 mph down the New Jersey Turnpike. After three hours of agony, I arrived in Baltimore.

When I got to Tanisha's grandmother's house, I was too nervous to get out of the car. Reggie stood on the porch. Finally, I found the courage to move. When Reggie saw me, he began shaking his head. I rushed up the steps.

"Reggie, what's going on?"

He hugged me and wept on my shoulder like a baby. "Clark."

Unsure of why, I cried, too. "Reggie, where is Tanisha?"

"That crazy bastard killed her. He killed her." He let go of me and fought the air. "He fucking killed her."

I screamed, "No! No!" I started hitting Reggie. "Who killed her, Reggie? Who?"

"Fred's crazy ass."

My hands covered my ears as I shook my head uncontrollably. In the middle of my tantrum, my body just stopped. I struggled to breathe. Every limb on my body was excessively heavy. Like someone was choking me, I gasped for air. I wanted to die, too. Why did He have to take Tanisha from me? I couldn't survive without her.

Finally, air passed through my lungs again. "Why? Why would he kill her?"

I grabbed at Reggie's shirt and shook him. He was to blame. He should have never left her. I yelled at him. "It's all your fault. She didn't deserve this. Why?"

He tried holding my wrist, but I fought to be released. He pleaded, "Clark, I know."

Everyone rushed from the house to drag me inside. I wailed, "Why?"

They all looked at me with sympathy, but no one answered. I yelled, "Somebody, tell me why the fuck did he kill my sister? I'm gonna kill 'em. I swear I'm gonna kill 'em."

I flung my body around, confused about my own existence. Before I knew it, I was stretched out in the living room, banging on the floor. Finally, my mother leaned down, wrapped her arms around me, and helped me to my feet. We walked into the kitchen. She whispered in my ear as we walked, "You don't have to kill him. The fool killed himself."

More confusion, "What would make him do that?"

"Baby, some people are sick. Fred was a sick man."

"What happened? What made him kill her? There are a lot of sick people, but they don't go around killin' people. Not people they're supposed to love."

She began, "Clark, when the investigators checked the scene, they found video cameras all over the house."

What did that have to do with anything? She hushed me before I could ask. She continued, "The neighbors heard arguing, then three shots fired. After they called the police, another shot was fired. They assumed the fourth shot was Fred killing himself. When the cops arrived, there was a video in the VCR." She closed her eyes tightly and took a deep breath. "A tape of Tanisha and Reggie having sex on Christmas Eve."

I yelled, "No!"

My best friend was gone because my brother was too selfish to let her go. "Why didn't he just let her move on with her life?" Totally ignoring my mother's presence, "Why was he still fucking her?"

My mother immediately defended Reggie. "Clark, don't go blaming Reggie for this. No matter what you or anybody thinks, he loved Tanisha. That's why he couldn't let her go." She continued, "People cheat all the time. It takes a sick person to tape you and kill you."

I shook my head. "Where are the babies?"

"I took them to Penny's house. They were with me when it happened. Thank God."

I snuggled up on my mother and wailed. How could someone love you and refuse to be with you? Love should be simple. Be with who you love, not the one that society thinks you should love.

What a tragic way to die. He shot her in her chest two times and once in her face with a .357 Magnum. Her beautiful face blown away. The only thing she ever did wrong in her life was love Reggie. The dedicated heart of a woman never gets its proper rewards.

Love is such a fragile word. The three most important people in my life lied to me all in the name of love. Two of them were gone forever. Can someone really love you so much that they are forced to deceive you? Doesn't it cause less pain in the end when you are honest?

Fuck love. In the end, no solution works. It's a crazy game for fools, and I quit.

THREE YEARS LATER

41

DEVIN

After being single for a year, I looked back over my life. I went from being madly in love with Clark to walking down the aisle with Jennifer. Overall, I can't complain. However, I wish I would've made wiser decisions.

After we got married, we moved into a two-bedroom condo in Midtown Manhattan. We agreed to raise our family in New York. Working for my parents' firm was no longer a part of my plan. In fact, I think it worked out ten times better.

Jennifer and I played house to the best of our ability, but there was always something missing. Nicole, our little girl, brought temporary satisfaction to our relationship. I never dreamed that I would love a child so much. When I saw Nicole, I never wanted to leave her. When Jennifer gave birth, I was delighted that I made her my wife. I thought God had it all planned for me.

The first year of Nicole's life, we were distracted by her presence. All we talked about was the baby. We didn't have to face the reality that we were never really in love. Once we graduated and began studying for the bar, we began to stress each other out. She felt like I wasn't doing enough to help her around the house. I felt like she was a pain in the ass. Many nights, I longed for the only other woman I knew, Clark. I wondered how things would be if I had never gotten Jennifer pregnant. I questioned my decision almost every day of my marriage. Then I would look into little Nicole's eyes and believe I made the right choice.

After I began practicing, I worked twelve to fifteen hours a day. I'd often come home and my baby girl was asleep. The only person to greet me was Jennifer. She wasn't enough. Arguments were frequent. We were both miserable, but determined to stay for the baby. In retrospect, I don't understand why people stay in turmoil and convince themselves they are staying for the baby. If anything, the tension in the house has more of a negative effect on the child. We didn't know any better. We were both fortunate enough to come from two-parent households, and we wanted to give our daughter the same. We pressed on, trying to make it work.

I would probably still be there, but one morning I inadvertently forgot to change the radio station in the car. She listens to country music. I, on the other hand, I have to listen to hip-hop to get through the day in a white man's world. This morning in particular, I was on the cell phone with a coworker. After hanging up, I became distracted by traffic. I found myself laughing as I casually listened to the callers. The topic was telling your deepest, darkest secrets. It began to amuse me. My mouth dropped to the floor of my Benz CLK 420 when Jennifer's voice came through the speakers. I turned up the volume.

"Yes, I'm calling to tell you my secret."

Jennifer has a dark secret? I continued to listen, just to get a clearer picture of the woman I was sleeping with every night.

Anxious to hear her story, the radio host cheered her on. "Okay, spill the tea!"

She cleared her throat. "Well, when I met my husband." She paused. My heart skipped a beat. It scared me to think that whatever she was about to say had something to do with me.

She continued, "I was instantly attracted to him. I wanted him by any means necessary. At the time, he had a girlfriend, who he really loved. So, we became close friends. The problem is I became more and more attracted to him."

The host eagerly awaited the next part. "Okay, so what happened?"

"He and his girlfriend broke up. We became sexually active,

and we, well, he decided we should take our time. In my heart, I knew he still loved his ex-girlfriend. After a week or so of sleeping with him, I knew I wanted him to be my husband. So, I poked holes in all of his condoms."

I yelled, "You bitch!!"

I wanted to turn around, go home, and strangle her.

The host laughed. "And did you get pregnant?"

She giggled, like my life was a damn game. "Yep. Faster than what I expected."

"So, one more question. Was it worth it?"

She took a breath. "Um, we're both miserable. So, I'd say no."

My palms were sweating. I literally felt like killing her. I wanted to murder my parents for convincing me that I should marry her sneaky ass. I reflected back on poor Clark, how terribly I had treated her, because I thought Jennifer was too innocent to hurt. How stupid! I walked into the office like someone had robbed me of my sanity.

In my morning meeting, I sat totally disturbed by the truth. Finally, I couldn't take it anymore. I went into my office, closed the door, and called Jennifer.

She answered with her innocent voice. "Yes, honey?"

I had planned to call her and curse her out tactfully, but I couldn't resist. I went off, "You bitch!! You sorry bitch!"

She tried to maintain her innocence. "Devin, what is wrong with you?"

"Bitch! I don't believe your ass."

"What are you talking about?"

"I heard your freak-ass on the radio this morning!"

Her voice began to quiver. "Devin, whatever! I don't even listen to the same station you listen to. So I know you didn't hear me on the radio."

"Naw, bitch, I was listening to your station! You fucking trapped me. You knew I loved Clark and you trapped me. I trusted your sorry ass."

She was crying at this point, apparently feeling stupid for revealing her deep, dark secret on the air. She would have never thought I'd be listening to that station. It was no coincidence.

God was showing me that the devil has a plan for your life, too. She was the wolf in sheep's clothing.

"Devin, I swear I wasn't on the radio. What are you talking about?"

"Why the fuck are you crying if it wasn't you?" For a second, I wanted to believe that maybe someone else sounded just like my wife. Then I wondered how many people with the same voice had the same exact story, probably zero. So I continued to light into her.

"I know it was you. You don't have to lie anymore. Fuck it. Like you said, we're both miserable. When I get home, I'm packin' my shit!"

She pleaded, "Devin, please. I love you."

"You don't love me. You manipulated me. You lied to me. That shit ain't love."

I hung up.

I called my secretary and told her that I wasn't taking any calls from my wife. Finally, after about an hour, my secretary called to tell me my wife was in the lobby. I asked her to make up something. Not on my job where I was making a name for myself. I wasn't going to give her two opportunities to screw up my life.

Talking to me wasn't going to change the way I felt. I sat at my desk all day, staring out of the window thinking about how much of a fool I'd been. Jennifer had always tried to convince me that a condom burst one time, but I could never recollect the occurrence. We had sex so much during that period, I honestly couldn't remember. I didn't think she was sleeping with anyone else, so I trusted that the baby was mine, and a DNA test proved my paternity. I never inquired again about the condom bursting. Jennifer wanted to have sex every hour on the hour when we first met. After Nicole was born, I'd be lucky to get it once a month.

I started calling different apartments to find a place to stay. I refused to sleep in the bed with her for another night. I wanted to take my little girl and fly miles away from that evil witch. I researched about getting custody of my baby. By the end of the day, my entire escape plan was mapped out.

When I walked in the house that evening, she was conducting

business as usual. She had dinner ready, and Nicole was running around screaming. When I walked in the kitchen, she looked up at me like she had accepted I was leaving.

"Devin, that wasn't me on the radio." She was still lying. If I had questioned my departure, her lies extinguished any doubt. "But, if you want to leave, do what you have to do."

I knew at that point, she had taken time to reflect, and like she said on the radio, it wasn't worth it. Jennifer saw me as the perfect guy, and she jumped through hoops to get me, only to realize I am just a man.

After a few angry, bitter weeks, I calmed down and accepted my idiocy. I peacefully wrote an effective separation agreement. We now have joint custody of Nicole. She stays with Jennifer from Monday to Thursday and with me on weekends.

The divorce was final just last week. I must say that a year alone has taught me so much about life. It was hard to see the big picture while trapped in any relationship.

I've dated several women over the past year; still, no one compares to the woman I abandoned three years ago. I often think about Clark. Would she have me back? If I could rewind and we could live happily ever after, I would do it in a heartbeat.

42

CLARK

After Tanisha's funeral, I moved in with my mother. I took a leave of absence from my job for three months. When I thought I was mentally healthy, I moved back into my own place. Morgan came with me. She refused to live in New York with Reggie and Sheena. She was mature enough to see that Sheena was her mother's rival. Little Reggie doesn't know any better. He wanted to be with his dad. Sheena and Reggie got married as planned. She's pregnant with their first baby. She called the wedding off when she first found out about the murder, but eventually took Reggie back out of sympathy.

After Morgan and I moved out, we both were still relatively distraught. We would crawl in the bed together after she finished her homework and watch movies all evening. I was helping my poor young niece slip deeper into depression, instead of finding coping solutions.

Eventually, I realized that I needed to get help if I planned to raise Morgan the way I knew Tanisha would want. It took me months to accept that I had literally had a nervous breakdown.

I went to the Agape Mental Health Center. At first, I felt funny going somewhere for help. During my first visit, a counselor spoke with me and highly recommended that the director counsel me. She took me to his office. When I walked in, I almost fainted. Kenneth Winston, a guy whom I've always referred to as my biggest regret at Hampton. Kenneth was still sexy and charming as ever. He was a senior when I was a freshman. I wanted to approach him from the moment I met him, but intimidation stopped me. During the spring semester, we had a class together and became friends. I didn't have the nerve to tell him that I wanted his body. Finally, a few days before he graduated, we both expressed our desires. We decided to fulfill our needs. I crept over to his apartment. We passionately indulged in foreplay. Just when I got to the point where I was about to explode, he pulled it out and reached for a condom. He fumbled. No condoms. It simply ruined the moment. Reluctantly, we both forced ourselves to fall asleep. Disgusted with his lack of preparation, I didn't exchange contact information. Looking back on it, I wondered why we didn't try other avenues to getting a condom, but we just left well enough alone. I had not seen him since the morning after the incident.

I stood there when the counselor introduced us, like I'd never seen him in my life. She left the room. "I'll leave you all to get acquainted."

Embarrassed that our reunion was under those circumstances, I hung my head. He smiled.

"Clark, girl, give me a hug." He grabbed me and held me tightly. He felt warm and strong, just as I remembered.

"Hey, Kenneth."

"So what brings you here?"

I sat down and told him about the dramatic journey that I'd faced over that past year. He listened and spoke only when necessary. We almost immediately began to bond. This time the connection was more intense than when we were in college.

We met frequently and it became obvious that we were embarking on a relationship. He questioned his judgment. How could he fall for a patient? We both tried to resist, but feelings grew stronger. I ended my therapy and we began to date.

Initially it was challenging, because he has custody of his ten-year-old daughter Mia and I had Morgan. Neither of us felt comfortable bringing the other around the girls until we were sure that the relationship was stable. As time passed, his sincerity and understanding freed my caged heart. Ready to love again. He was everything I needed to get my life in order. After eight months or so, we allowed the girls to meet. From the moment they met, they loved each other. It was like a reincarnation of Tanisha and me. Their closeness brought my heart joy and peace. The union is ordained.

Kenneth came into my life to heal my pain. I often reflect on what I felt for Devin and wonder if it really was love. I spent so much time trying to be perfect that I lost sight of me. With Kenneth, I am just Clark. I don't have to suppress my urban habits. He loves me just because.

Kenneth has taught me so much about life and relationships. I don't know where I'd be if it wasn't for his therapy. He has truly given me peace. When he asked me to be his wife, I knew it was right.

I had felt like my world was crashing down on me, but I think that it was God's way of grabbing my attention so I could receive the blessing he had for me.

After the wedding, my only job would be supporting Kenneth at the clinic. On my last day at the office, I sifted through my junk before I threw it all away. I sat at my desk and sorted through the piles of paper. I found dozens of letters and poems that I had written to Devin. I ripped them to tiny pieces and threw them in the trash, along with the leftover emotions.

Grateful that I'd finally found true happiness and ended my depression, I let a tear roll from my eye, a single tear of joy for a beginning and an ending. I sat there, reminiscing on my life before Kenneth, back when I thought love was this constant high. I chuckled at my immaturity, and the phone rang.

"MICROS, Clark speaking."

The person on the other end paused. "Hello, Ms. Anderson, this is . . ." He paused.

I knew who it was. I almost dropped the phone.

"An old friend."

Pretending the voice didn't faze me, I asked, "Who am I speaking with?"

"Devin Patterson." He sounded so formal. Why was he calling?

My heart began to flutter, because we always had that tenacious chemistry. Whenever I thought of him, he'd call and vice versa.

After hours of relationship courses that taught me to let go in love, I still felt angry. It all went out of the door. I coaxed myself, "Clark, you are better, not bitter."

I forced a pleasant greeting. "Hey, Devin. How's everything?"

He chuckled. "Clark, I really don't know where to begin."

Although I was anxious to hear why he was calling, I tried to appear cool. "Just tell me how life's been treating you."

"Life has been fucked up ever since I left you."

Pleased that he was apparently miserable in his marriage, I unsympathetically said, "Oh, well, that's the way love goes sometimes. How's Jennifer? And the baby? What did you guys have?"

As the words came out, visions of the woman who stole my man came to mind. I couldn't give a damn about her or the baby they conceived.

"We had a girl. And Jennifer, she's fine." He took a breath. "We're divorced."

I hate the thought of marriages ending, but I felt a sense of gratitude. "Really, why?"

"I made the wrong decision."

Did he expect a reaction? "Yeah, it happens like that sometimes."

Cutting to the chase, "Clark, I'm in town for a few days. Can I take you to dinner?"

First of all, he assumed I was still available. I laughed softly. I thought about how he had blatantly told me that he didn't love me anymore. With strong emphasis, I said, "Nope."

Stunned by my negative vibe, he stuttered a little. "Huh . . . c'mon. Clark, please. I really need to see you and apologize. Not a day went by that I didn't think of you."

My turn for rejection had arrived. "Oh, really. I think you're a little too late."

"I just want to talk."

"Honestly, Devin, I have nothing to say to you. I cried for almost a year after we broke up. I almost lost my mind, not to mention my job, all because of you. All because you didn't think I was good enough. I spent months questioning myself, doubting myself. I could never forgive you for all the emotional anguish you caused me."

Apparently surprised at his effect on me, "Clark, I had no idea that I hurt you that bad. I made a mistake. I never stopped loving you and you know it."

"I came and begged you not to marry Jennifer. And if I recall correctly, you said you didn't love me. So, I don't *know* anything. I do know that I don't love you anymore."

He still had a hold on me, because I didn't hang up like I planned. It disturbed me that I wasn't tough enough to just end the conversation.

"Clark. I'm sorry that I caused you so much pain, but I know I made the wrong decision. I just want you to hear me out. I need to see you and tell you everything."

What did he want to say? I knew it wasn't wise to see him. I struggled with my feelings. Something in me still cared about him. Why weren't the feelings gone? My heart told me to go and be sure that I was ready to move on. What were the chances that he called on my last day? Wanting to believe it was a sign, when it was a mere coincidence, I snapped out of my stupidity. Devin is not worth losing the man who saved me from destruction.

"Devin, I really don't care how you feel. I wish you the best. I am sorry that you made the wrong decision, but I can't be the one to rescue you. Those days are over. I hope you have a good life."

I courageously hung up the receiver. I threw all the papers piled on my desk in the trash. I had no desire to face the memories. It was my past. I was about to marry the man of my dreams. I stared at the phone number I scribbled down from the caller ID and mumbled, "Good-bye, Devin Patterson."

CAUGHT IN THE MIX

CANDICE DOW

ABOUT THIS GUIDE

The suggested questions are intended
to enhance your group's reading
of Candice Dow's book.

DISCUSSION QUESTIONS

1. Did Clark make the right decision to stay in Maryland?
2. If Clark hadn't gone to France, how do you think Devin planned to handle the introduction with Clark and his parents?
3. Was Devin more afraid of being cut off financially from his parents or of losing Clark?
4. Were Clark's expectations of a first-year law student unreasonable? In fact, were her expectations in general unreasonable?
5. Were Devin's reasons for keeping his relationship and his family separate justified?
6. Were Devin's issues with being biracial realistic?
7. Was it fair for Clark to keep her pregnancy a secret and make the decision to abort without Devin's consent?
8. Did her decision to have an abortion validate her love for Devin or invalidate her love for herself?
9. Should Tanisha have gotten so serious with a man that she knew couldn't take Reggie's place? Is it better to deal with the pain until the right guy comes along or to find anyone to get you over that someone?
10. Why did Clark feel so insecure with Devin's parents? What outside factors contributed to her lack of confidence?
11. What were some of Jennifer's traits that could have possibly convinced Devin she was better than Clark?
12. Knowing that Tanisha did not love Fred, what could Clark have done to make her best friend see the light? Or did she handle it appropriately?
13. Could Clark share the blame for the failure of the relationship? Did it appear she ever took responsibility?
14. When two people choose to go separate ways, why is closure important? What stops couples from getting that closure?

15. Did Reggie actually live two separate lives? How could Tanisha be so certain that it was love between them?
16. Is it possible to love two people? And what factors outweigh others when a choice has to be made?
17. What type of issues could Morgan have from the tragic death of her mother? Will those issues be the same for little Reggie?
18. Is it possible that Clark has really opened up to love again?